A BAD MAN'S COMEUPPANCE

Zack Queen stumbled through the shattered doorway. Kind of appeared out of a billowing cloud of dust, like magic. I made the mistake of standing to get a better shot. Hymn-singing drunk rubber-legged his way straight for me, and sprayed a wall of lead from an iron-framed Henry rifle. Second or third one cut a hole in my pistol belt and burned through my side like a Civil War surgeon's scalpel. Knocked me flat on my back, and rendered me helpless as a week-old babe.

Ole Zack staggered all the way to the bottom of the hill, came to a wobbling stop over my poor bleeding ass and yelped, "Well, Tilden, you goddamned do-rights might want to say a prayer or two, 'cause it's time to shake hands with Jesus."

Then he leveled that Henry up, and managed to take aim at the biggest part of me before Carlton put one in the drunken bastard's fogged-up noggin that went in one side and pushed most of his brain out the other. Brains, blood, and all manner of gore splattered right in my face. Messy business for damned sure.

BROTHERHOOD OF BLOOD

J. LEE BUTTS

BERKLEY BOOKS, NEW YORK

BROTHERHOOD OF BLOOD

A Berkley Book / published by arrangement with
the author

PRINTING HISTORY
Berkley edition / March 2004

Copyright © 2004 by J. Lee Butts.
Cover illustration by Bruce Emmitt.
Cover design by Jill Boltin.

ISBN: 0-425-19481-7

BERKLEY®
Berkley Books are published by The Berkley Publishing Group,
a division of Penguin Group (USA) Inc.,
375 Hudson Street, New York, New York 10014.
BERKLEY and the "B" design
are trademarks belonging to Penguin Group (USA) Inc.

PRINTED IN THE UNITED STATES OF AMERICA

10 9 8 7 6 5 4 3 2

For Carol
Whose patience and support continue to amaze me

and

Roxanne Blackwell Bosserman
Whose heartfelt encouragement has kept me going long past
the time when many friends have wavered

ACKNOWLEDGMENTS

A big tip of the sombrero and bow from the waist to Michael and Barbara Rosenberg for their continuing efforts on my behalf. Special thanks to Kimberly Lionetti for all her help and understanding. And finally, as always, my limitless gratitude to every member of the DFW Writer's Workshop for a weekly dose of the kind of knowledge, experience, and advice money can't buy.

ACKNOWLEDGMENTS

When you are about to drink a glass of whiskey, look closely in the bottom and see if you cannot observe therein a hangman's noose. There is where I first saw the one that now breaks my neck.

> Boudinot (Bood) Crumpton
> Youngest man hanged at Fort Smith
> Gates of Hell, October 1, 1890

Beware of strong drink, for it alone is responsible for my present condition.

> John Thornton
> Oldest man hanged at Fort Smith
> Gates of Hell, June 28, 1892

Pale death treads with even steps the hovels of the poor and the palaces of kings.

> From the first book of Horace
> Scribbled note found in the
> pocket of Arliss (Barefoot)
> Stackpole, murdered by Zack
> Queen, 1883

PROLOGUE

WELL, NOW, LET'S get this manhunt moving. I'd just got back to Fort Smith from a trip to the Choctaw Nation. Been out trying to catch L. B. Ledoux. Ended up having to kill the stupid bastard.

Truth is, I only went out on that raid by accident. Deputy by the name of Jasper Fowler caught me, and some others, loafing around Marshal Valentine Dell's outer office one cool spring morning. He sidled up, straddled a chair, and said, "Gotta make a run over to Blue Mountain. Any you boys wanna string along?"

Must have been six or eight of those who rode for Judge Parker, whittling, spitting, and telling lies that morning. But none of the congregation jumped up and volunteered to help ole Jasper. Didn't take long 'fore I got to feeling right sorry for the man.

"Come on now, fellers. Know it ain't much, but I don't wanna make this here trip alone." Sounded like he was about to break down and cry there for a second or two.

Can't remember who finally spoke up, but one of the more devoutly worshipful said, "Who're you going out for this time, Jasper?"

Fowler scratched a match to life and lit a hand-rolled. "L. B. Ledoux." He blew smoke toward the ceiling and spit a sprig of tobacco into our growing pile of pine shavings.

Took a spell, but the next question to bubble up came from Trapper Starks. "What'd the sorry son of a bitch do to warrant our attention—again?"

"Stole a horse. Maybe more'n one. Farmer over in the Nations by the name of Boston missed at least one of his'n. He filed the complaint. Need another man, maybe two, to stroll down with me and gather L. B. up. Won't take more'n four or five days over, and as many to get back. Guaranteed money. Know exactly where the thievin' bastard's located. Won't even have to chase him any. Just bring him in and collect."

Should've paid closer attention. Wasn't thinking straight that morning, I guess. Felt sorry for Jasper and raised my hand. "Don't have anything going on right now myself. Always liked Blue Mountain. Beautiful place up there this time of year. Nice, easy ride. We'll just mosey down his way and drag ole L. B. back, Jasper. Find out what Judge Parker has in store for him. Year or two up in the Detroit Correctional Facility shouldn't do him any harm."

Billy Bird shaved off another sliver from what he said was going to be a bust of Robert E. Lee. "If Hayden's going, you can count me in." He shot me a sneaky grin and winked. "It'll be fun."

Foggy as my antiquated mind's become, I can still see Elizabeth standing on the porch next morning, waving good-bye. She's probably the most vivid piece of that particular recollection. Seems like memories of hearth and home tend to jump out at you later when things go horribly wrong.

Jasper, Billy, and me had an uneventful trip. Just meandered along and enjoyed ourselves immensely. Stopped a few times on the way and went fishing in Caney Creek. Caught a big ole catfish that must've weighed near ten pounds. Mighty fine eating.

Found Ledoux's shack three days or so after we crossed the Arkansas and punched into the Kiamichi Mountains. L. B. kept company with a Choctaw gal named Mary White Leg. Every tobacco-chewing plow pusher within five miles of their cabin knew where the couple stayed.

Their combination farm and horse-selling operation occupied a mountainside spot that looked down on mist-covered rolling foothills. Had the kind of view people today would pay a handsome price for. Soon as we rode into the chicken-shit-covered yard, things went sour in a damned big hurry.

Billy noted there weren't any animals to be seen. Under his breath, he mumbled my direction, "Shade strange for a horse operation not to have any horses available, ain't it?"

Jasper jumped off his mount, stomped up onto the cluttered porch, and started banging at the door like a man possessed. Cannot to this very minute imagine what in the blue-eyed hell he thought he was doing. Seemed to me a damned stupid act, then and now. Maybe he just

wanted to show off or something. Could be that was the
way he always did his business. Never heard anyone else
comment on one side of the question or the other.
Damned sure didn't get a chance to ask Jasper.

He whacked the door some more and started yelling,
"Get your sorry thievin' ass out here, Ledoux. I'm a
deputy U.S. marshal from Judge Parker's court in Fort
Smith, you horse-stealing son of a bitch. Have a bona
fide warrant for your arrest. Open up, goddammit."

Got mighty quiet for a second or so. Billy said,
"Don't like the looks of this a bit, Hayden. Something's
not right here."

Jasper stood spraddle-legged with his fists on his hips.
Man vibrated like a picked banjo string. He grunted and
grinned at us over his shoulder. Then he kicked the hell
out of the rickety door. He'd booted the grimy slats four
or five times when a shotgun blast from inside ripped a
hole in those rough planks and punched a cavern the
size of my fist in his heaving chest. Tightly bunched wad
of twelve-gauge shot pushed the moon-and-star-shaped
badge out his back in a knot of blood, bone, and metal.
Knocked him ten feet. Boy flew like a corn-shuck doll
caught in a cyclone of spraying gore. Hit the ground
right at my horse Gunpowder's feet. The sorrel gelding
spooked and started bucking. You'd a thought he had a
grass burr the size of a bucket up his butt.

As that big, rough beast twirled, bounced, and hopped
around the barnyard, Billy whipped out both his Schofield .45s and blasted the front of Ledoux's shack so fast
the gunfire sounded like one continuous explosion. In
spite of considerable concentration on trying my level
best to stay in the saddle, I could hear people yelling
and screaming behind the bullet-riddled walls. Sounded
like Billy might have put holes in at least two of 'em.

Once I got control of Gunpowder again, we managed to make safety behind a stand of trees about a hundred feet from where Jasper gushed the rest of his short, stupid life into the ground. Pulled rifles, shotguns, and extra ammunition on the run.

Billy signaled his intention to circle the cabin and cover any attempted escape from the back. Left me in charge of everything out front—including Jasper's twitching corpse. Only good part of the whole deal lay in a fluke of topography. Timber cover, and Ledoux's shack, occupied the same level of a stumpy, flattened hill. Leastways we weren't below any shooters Billy'd accidentally left alive.

Had barely got myself settled and primed when a woman I assumed was Mary White Leg stepped out on the cabin's ramshackle porch. "We have wounded in here, marshals. Some of the men are in a bad way."

Billy hadn't built his nest exactly where he wanted yet. From behind a lightning-splintered oak on the west side of Ledoux's crude dwelling, he yelled, "Tell 'em to throw down their weapons and come out, one at a time, with their hands in the air, palms up. Any more treachery from the ambushing bastards and we'll kill every man in there."

Got no way of knowing exactly what she intended. People often do strange things when folks around them commence dying in violent ways. Mary White Leg ducked her head and started down the steps. Heard a man's strangled voice from behind what was left of the perforated door. Couldn't tell exactly what was said at first.

Voice kept getting louder. Finally he screamed, "Come back here, woman. Get back in this house, right goddamned now." She just kept on a-hoofin' it. Never looked back. Made it about ten feet past Jasper's oozing carcass. Then she looked up at me like she thought I could help her.

For a second or so our eyes met. She was scared to death. I could see it on her face. Rifle shot from the doorway brought her down. She held most of a shattered heart in blood-soaked hands when she hit the ground. Ended up on her knees—a strange, crooked statue of death that leaned but never fell.

Billy and I both cut loose with everything we had. Might've only been two of us, but that makeshift hut rattled and shook like we were cranking a Gatling gun. Not much of a place to hide when you're behind single-plank walls.

Screaming and whooping from inside started all over again. Since we could pour lead directly in on them, the scum-sucking dogs didn't have a chance. Especially with Deputy Marshal Billy Bird blasting away. Sweet William had an amazing knack for putting holes in bad men—even when he couldn't see them.

Two of us made things so hot inside that tinderbox of Ledoux's, guess them ole boys just couldn't stand the heat. Three men broke for freedom. Dumb bastards almost made it to the woods. But they headed right into a wall of pistol fire. Don't think I'd ever seen grown men do anything quite so stupid up till then. Billy Bird stepped from behind his tree and blew 'em out of their well-worn boots—easy as eating apple pie on Sunday.

Got mighty quiet once the gunfire finally died down. We waited almost an hour, and nothing else happened. Not a sound. Right eerie, after all the shouting, shooting, and dying that'd gone on just previous. Made my skin crawl.

Body count outside came to one of us and four of

them—if you included that poor dead woman. Not a hint available as to what awaited us inside. And to tell the righteous truth, I didn't look forward to finding out.

Eventually Billy made his way back to my hidey-hole. We talked it over and decided to rush whoever might be left. Got onto the wobbly veranda without incident—still no sound or movement. Surprised us when we burst inside with our shotguns cocked and ready to deal out more death and destruction. No one there.

Marshal Bird stood in the middle of swirling dust, broken dishes, busted furniture, and a pile of used whiskey bottles. He said, "Musta got all 'em, Hayden."

Place was emptier than a rain barrel in Arizona. They'd all come out the front because L. B. Ledoux, who evidently wasn't much at building houses, hadn't bothered to put a back door in the place.

Billy said, "Too damned stupid to take a shotgun and blow a hole in the wall. God Almighty, people this dumb don't need to be using up my air."

Couldn't help but add my two pennies' worth. "Hate these goddamned whiskey-swilling bastards, Marshal Bird. Judge Parker's right. Damned stuff they drink is nothing but a 'fruitful source of evil, disorder, and criminal activity—a many-headed demon.' "

As it turned out, Ledoux was one of the dumber-than-a-fencepost runners Billy put down when they hoofed it for the briars and brambles. Two of them ole boys managed to still be alive in spite of being shot up pretty good.

For reasons known only to a benevolent God, Jumpin' Joe Moody and Rufus Low Dog didn't succumb to unknowable internal injuries, colossal blood loss, our questionable medical efforts, or rampant infection. Sons of bitches lived, and made it back to Fort Smith for trial.

Hell, maybe the whiskey saved 'em. Who knows?

Some damned good lawyers got 'em off, too. Claimed those boys hadn't stole anything. Didn't have the slightest idea who we were. Whole bloody mess got heaped on Ledoux's poor dead noggin. He killed Jasper, they said. Shot his wife, too, according to their highly questionable testimony. That's the story they told. And it worked. Damned soft-headed juries turned 'em loose.

The nightmares started right after that. In the dream, I saw Mary White Leg's face as clear as if she were standing in front of me this instant. She ran toward me. Hope took over, and she smiled. Second later, most of her face disappeared behind a cloud of scarlet vapor gushing from her chest. Gory vision had the power to snap me upright like someone standing at the foot of my bed had cracked a muleskinner's bullwhip deep inside my brain.

Thank God that particular horror stayed with me but a short time. 'Bout midway through Rufus Low Dog's day in court, I dragged Zack Queen back to Fort Smith and Carlton J. Cecil started us on the gruesome path to the Brotherhood of Blood. Never had another dream about Mary White Leg after we went out searching for Precious Tall Dog. Horrors of that hunt blotted out damned near everything else for years to come.

1
"Rancid Body Popped to the Surface"

IN THE SUMMER of '48 I'll just be damned if Franklin J. Lightfoot Jr. didn't make good on his threat about dragging my ancient moss-covered ass out to Hollywood, Cali-damn-fornia, to talk movie deals with A. Maxwell Vought. Junior made out like it was my eighty-ninth birthday present.

Our own personal big-time producer and self-styled mogul paid all the freight for Frank, nurse Heddy McDonald, and me. Flew us out on an airplane no less. Put us up in a joint looked like a whorehouse called the Beverly Hills Hotel. I cared not one damned bit for that flying part of the deal.

Day after we arrived Maxwell treated us to breakfast at a place named the Polo Lounge. Soon's I'd had three of them drinks called Bloody Marys, it didn't take me long to start telling tall ones. Hell, them movie people encouraged it. 'Specially a couple of damned good-looking gals at the table. Said they wanted to hear all my tales of the old west, hunting bad men and such. Ain't nothing like female flattery to loosen up an old man's lip.

The Brotherhood just kinda popped out. Hadn't meant to say anything concerning that particular experience. Actually came to talk about Frank's book, *Lawdog*. But the truth is, you just can't keep something as awful as the Brotherhood hidden forever. So, with a gallery of the blondest, tannest people alive hanging on my every word, I hit 'em with the stunning horror of the thing from beginning to end.

Studied my audience a bit, leaned back in the chair, and said, "I've never told anyone this bloody tale."

Been living on the ground for most of a month while I searched for Zack Queen. Murdering scum dispatched Arliss Stackpole in the most brutal fashion imaginable. Promised Judge Parker I'd kill Zack when I set out after him. Only managed to wound the murderous bastard a couple of times though, and had to drag his sorry ass back to Parker's two-room dungeon of a jail in Fort Smith.

Soon as I dropped the scurvy cur off and trudged upstairs to the U.S. marshal's office, Carlton J. Cecil grabbed me by the arm and pulled me over to the nearest corner. Been a long time since I'd seen Ole Carl that worked up about anything. He appeared more agitated than Billy Bird the time just before, during, and after we braced Jug Dudley and his bunch of lethal cowboys down in Black Oak, Texas.

Honest to God, it could be a mite scary when a man

like Carlton got so sparky. Whatever burr he had under
his saddle really had him humped up and kicking. Always got a charge out of Carlton when he boiled over
all hot and bothered that way. Nothing quite as amusing
as watching a heavily armed little pissant like him take
off on a real ripsnorter. Better than buying a ticket for
one of those traveling carnivals and monkey shows.

Knew he'd likely hit me with something so important
I probably wouldn't be able to refuse whatever request
he made. But hindsight being what it is, if me or any of
the rest of the men who ended up involved in that ugly
undertaking would've had any idea how dark, shocking,
and gruesome the hunt for Precious Tall Dog was gonna
turn out, we might have made our excuses and let someone else take the lead. Know for goddamned sure I
would've.

"Hayden, have you heard what them Crooke boys
from near Phantom Hill did?" Carlton hopped from foot
to foot. Swear he acted like a ten-year-old kid who had
red-hot money in his pocket and couldn't wait to get to
a hurdy-gurdy show that didn't pass through town but
once a year. And as far as he was concerned, the best
act in the whole deal just happened to be Nekkid Nadine
and her snake.

Seemed to me like I'd heard of the Crooke family,
but so far I'd never had any dealings with them. Held
on to a fairly vague idea where Phantom Hill might be.
"You mean that one-dog place over in the Choctaw Nation between Antlers and Atoka that can't even afford a
town drunk so everyone in the rustic berg takes a turn?
Barely a wide spot in a dirt road?" Tried to get a laugh
out of him, but he'd left his sense of humor somewhere
else that morning.

"Yeah, that's the one." He followed me around the

marshal's outer office, and we each pulled up a run-down chair and tried to get comfortable. Pistols and spurs got rearranged. Leaned my .45-70 Winchester against the wall in the nearest corner. Took my gun belt off and hung it over the cane-bottom's top rail, next to the Mexican rowels Ranger Lucius Dodge gave me before he hoofed it back to Texas.

"Haven't been privy to much of anything by way of news lately, Carlton, bad or otherwise. Been out in the wilds trying to run Zack Queen to ground. He's the sorry dung weevil that murdered Arliss Stackpole."

Carlton got a look on his face like he'd just turned a corner and stepped in something big and gooey left in the street by one of those draft horses used to pull beer wagons. He was shocked and amazed—pretty good trick for a man who'd seen and heard as much as he had.

"The traveling teacher? You mean *Barefoot* Stackpole, that young feller who preached some on the side and went around helping Indian kids learn how to read English?"

"You hit a bull's-eye there my friend."

"Damned if that don't show you how far back out in the sticks I've been for the past month. Hadn't even heard about his unfortunate departure from this life. Everybody who met the man liked ole Barefoot. You couldn't locate a finer feller in the Nations with a solid gold dowsing rod. It'd take a pretty sorry type to kill a man as exceptional as Arliss."

"Well, it seems Mr. Stackpole's final instructional efforts for the Creek Nation's young people took place over at Redbird near Okmulgee. Those fine folks paid him for his yearlong scholarly efforts with more than two hundred dollars in spanking new double eagle coins. Guess he made the mistake of letting Queen spot some of his stash when he stopped at Hildebrant's Store, before he barefooted his way out of town. Murdering ambusher caught the shoeless teacher out in the big cold and lonely with no one around. Shot the unarmed boy in the head a time or two."

"God Almighty!" Carlton bit off a ragged fingernail and spit it into the corner.

"That didn't come close to the worst of it, Carl. Naturally, he robbed the dead man, but took the dreadful extra step that separates run-of-the-mill killers from heartless butchers."

My old friend leaned forward in his chair and covered his eyes with his hands. "Damn, Hayden. Don't like the sound of this at all. Feels like lunacy of the first order is about to raise its ugly head and snap to attention."

"Yep, you're right, my friend. He cut the corpse open, pulled the innards out, stuffed the cavity full of rocks, and dumped the whole shebang into the Deep Fork of the Canadian, over close to Catfish Bend. Must have figured he'd covered the thing up pretty well. Couldn't have been any further off the mark on that one, though."

Carlton closed his eyes and shook his head like the weight of the world had fallen on him. "Sweet merciful Jesus, Hayden. Sometimes the insanity of the stuff we have to witness is enough to drive a man to heavy stagger juice consumption. Maybe even some of that bootleg Arkansas skull buster, so popular with folks out there in the Nations who seem determined to kill themselves with any kind of alcohol they can lay a quaking hand on."

For a few seconds he stared into my eyes like a man who'd lost his way and had difficulty clawing back to reality. "Honest to God, Hayden, the longer I live, the easier it is for me to understand why some men move into caves and become hermits. Makes a body wonder what in the blue-eyed hell the world is gonna be like a hundred years from now, if things keep going in the direction we're traveling."

"It is a mind-bending puzzler, Carl. Anyhow, guess ole Zack, the murdering polecat we were talking about before you got all spiritual on me, did a pretty sloppy job on what was left of Arliss. Rancid body popped to the surface downstream a day or two later, right in front of a bunch of kids playing on the bank while their mothers washed clothes.

"Several folks had seen Queen follow the luckless teacher from Hildebrant's. Didn't have to do much, in the way of serious detective work, figuring out who killed the man. Personally tried to rid the world of the scum-sucking slug's worthless shadow, but after I shot the slimy scalawag a time or two, he cried like a week-old baby and begged so pitiful I had to bring him back. No doubt in my mind, Judge Parker will convict him of murder most foul, and that the son of a bitch will swing from George Maledon's Gates of Hell gallows."

Carlton pushed his hat brim up against the crown. He kicked at an iron leg on the stove with the toe of his boot, shook his head again, and slipped into about a minute's worth of deep meditations, before he managed to say anything else. A philosophical sadness crept into his voice. The kind of sound that saturates a man's being when he feels like he's seen too much of the madness his fellow men are capable of setting loose on an unsuspecting world.

"Good God, but I am sorry to hear all that. And, trust me, I'm not trying to top your story here, Hayden, but about a week ago Myron Crooke, and his younger brother Byron, evidently got into a batch of bonded in the barn jig juice and went crazier'n a pair of turpentined cats. Folks who've done any thinking on the subject figure maybe the stuff was so hot, it burned up most of their pigeon-sized brains. We've had a few insignificant problems with 'em before. They've done some whiskey introducing off and on over the years, bit of livestock theft, drunken fistfight here and there—minor law breaking that never amounted to much. But this time around, they've evidently danced way over the line."

I scratched a match to life on the potbellied stove and fired up a fresh maduro panatela. Got the rum-soaked beast burning nicely and spit out an errant piece of tobacco before I asked, "How far over the line, Carlton?"

" 'Bout as far as our Texas Ranger amigo Lucius Dodge's cow pony, Hateful, could jump. Guess they'd been partaking of their various jugs of joy juice for a day or so, when the full effect of that rotgut hit 'em."

He puffed his own stogie to life off mine before the tale of murder and insanity continued. Savored a deep draw, then plowed back in. "Sometime late last Tuesday, them boys must've decided it'd been too long since they'd had the pleasant company and tender affections of a woman."

"Sweet merciful Jesus. Think I could probably tell where this one's going before you can get to the end of it."

"No, Hayden. In this particular bloody instance, don't think anyone could have foreseen what they were about to do, whether they had a crystal ball or a pack of them fortune-teller's cards. And, to be truthful, I'm not even sure exactly what all happened myself. Right now, the only things we know for certain are that Mary Beth Kincade Tall Dog, a widder woman who was once married to a Choctaw feller named Abraham Tall Dog, got her sad self murdered in some kind of lethally brutal fashion, and her thirteen-year-old daughter has gone missing. Folks who know the girl say she's quite a beauty. Physically, she got the absolute best of both worlds, from what I'm told. One of Bixley Conner's posse members claimed he saw the girl 'bout a year ago. Said she was the most beautiful female-type person he'd ever laid eyes on."

Thumped the ash from my smoke into the soot-and-cinder-covered tin tray under the stove. "Got to admit, Carlton, making off with the girl was bad, but not a completely new wrinkle. Can't remember hearing of a woman being stolen since the time Saginaw Bob Magruder and his bunch made off with Elizabeth. Molested, yes. Murdered, absolutely—especially if any molesting takes place before hand. But child stealing, that's a shocker. Sounds like white men taking up old Indian ways."

"Yeah. The Choctaw Light Horse Police wired the U.S. marshal from Tuskahoma. Those boys want some of us to get out to Phantom Hill as quick as we can, since they're not allowed do anything with white perpetrators but keep an eye on 'em. Have the warrants in my pocket. Wondered if you might like to go along with me on this one."

"Do you know our contact out there, Carl?"

"Yes, sir, I do. Worked with him several times. Name's Dennis Limber Hand—fine figure of a Choctaw feller. Educated in agency schools, even attended college back east. Hear tell he read for the law, but had to give it up for some reason. Intelligent, well spoken, you'll like him, Hayden."

I felt tired to the bone, wanted not to think of such

things, for a few hours anyway. Stood and started for the door. "Probably have to be in town for at least a day or two, what with depositions and all on Queen. On top of that, I haven't seen my wife or son in over a month. So, if you can wait around for a bit, we'll get out after those bad boys shortly, but I can't go right this minute."

"Hell, Hayden, I understand. You visit with Elizabeth and the boy. We'll hit the trail to Phantom Hill whenever you're ready to go. Ain't no rush. Limber Hand's doing what he can till we can get there."

Knew he didn't realize exactly what he'd said, but Carlton was as right as a barrel full of crystal-clear rainwater. My time at home had turned into brief, widely spaced visits that always ended with hugs, kisses, and tearful good-byes. Two years had passed since the notorious dustup in Red Rock Canyon, and during that entire span, I probably hadn't been able to spend more than three or four months with my family. Even missed the birth of my first son, Thomas Jefferson Tilden.

When Tommy made his debut, I'd been out in the land of the fuzztails, chasing after a sorry piece of humanity named Sinker Williams. Williams was meaner than five acres of snakes. Man had been arrested at least three times on a variety of violent accusations. Most brutal involved the time he attacked his common-law wife with a butcher's knife. Amanda Cold Woman survived some horrific wounds, even dropped the attempted murder charges, but a couple of years later disappeared, never to be seen or heard from again. Everyone knew he probably killed her, but no one was ever able to find a body. Turned over every rock within five miles of his ramshackle home and didn't come across so much as a wayward strand of hair.

I ended up chasing him, all over the Nations, because

he hid behind a rock near Sprague Simpson's place and planned to ambush the man. Sprague had given ole Sinker a severe head-and-shoulders beating after they disagreed over ownership of a horse. Seems Williams bought the animal from Simpson, but never bothered to pay for it. Guess Simpson must have got tired of waiting for his money.

About the time Sinker got settled into a comfortable ambush nest, his very best friend in the whole wide world, Jubilee Jefferson, just happened to ride by at the worst possible time and place he could have picked. Sinker evidently didn't give his victim much of a looking over before he started shooting. Blasted the hell out of the wrong cowboy. Put four .45-caliber slugs from a Winchester in ole Jubilee. Have to declare Sinker was one hell of a shot. All four were deadly, but most folks felt the one that hit Jefferson in the eye, and blew most of his brains into a bloody lump beside him on the ground, was the one that killed him.

At Sinker's trial, the nervy son of a bitch had his lawyer argue that he shouldn't be convicted because the murder was nothing more than an accident. According to them, it was simply a catastrophic case of mistaken identity. Jury didn't buy their sack of horseshit and laughed out loud for most of the five minutes it took them to find him guilty of murdering his best friend.

Judge Parker sentenced the malicious slug to a one-way visit with the executioner. Course ole Sinker's lawyer appealed the sentence. Didn't do much good. Supreme court denied it. Sinker complained like a sixty-year-old spinster and raised almighty hell right up to the end. Grim-faced executioner, Mr. Maledon, led him up to the Gates of Hell and dropped the trap on the murdering skunk so quick he was still protesting his innocence when he hit the end of a piece of well-oiled Kentucky hemp.

Fort Smith New Era reported his final words were something along the lines of, ' It were just a mistake. Jubilee were my best friend and boon companion. Never would've shot him if'n I'd of . . ' ' Thump from the trap, and a broken neck that snapped like a green cottonwood limb, drowned out anything else he might have had to say on the subject. Most folks were sick and tired of listening to him whine anyhow.

Thank God my wife, Elizabeth, was an understanding woman. Think I'd probably just tried to bend my pistol barrel over Sinker's petrified noggin when Tommy made it clear he was ready to start his screaming entrance into this world. Elizabeth got Judith Cecil, and some of her other friends, to come over and help with the birthing.

Actually, turned out a good thing Carlton and I couldn't be there for the delivery. Back in them days having a man around when a baby got born was about as smart as playing Russian roulette with a single-shot pistol. Having Carlton J. Cecil around anything like a baby's birth held the potential for screaming fits, nervous breakdowns, heavy-duty spider killer consumption, and possible murder.

By the time I finally got back to Fort Smith the boy was almost a month old. As I rode up to the house, my beautiful wife stood on the front steps of the veranda we had built around our entire home, and held Tommy up so I could see him from almost a mile away.

My knowledge of babies suffered considerably. Showed up at home that day carrying presents, of course—jeans big enough for a ten-year-old and a pair of boots that would have fit Billy Bird. Don't think a happier man lived when she lowered Tommy's squirming, pink body into my open arms. Carlton said I smiled like an escaped mental patient for over a week.

During the year that had passed, I still hadn't managed to spend enough time with the boy to make it possible for me to pick him out of a lineup of baby criminals. Every time I did get to stay at home for a few days, it always amazed me how much he'd grown and, not surprisingly, how much he looked like his mother. Swear the older she got the more striking Elizabeth became. Exactly the opposite of what happened with most women out on the frontier and in the wild places. Hard living had the power to turn females, once thought of as beauties, into wrinkled-up, weather-beaten old crones— but not my Elizabeth.

Left Carlton sitting in the marshal's office chewing on the remnants of his cigar. Walked Gunpowder up Towson Avenue to Elizabeth's store. Fort Smith had changed quite a bit since my arrival back in '79. Seemed like a new retail business, bakery, saloon, cafe, or dance hall of some kind opened almost every day.

Those were quickly matched by an equal number of new *boarding*houses—most popular of which belonged to a lady named Lilly Belle Squires. From what I heard, Lilly Belle's place, located a few blocks from the Frisco rail yards, sported Oriental carpets, crystal chandeliers, and ice-cold champagne for the high-toned types who held their pinkie fingers out when they drank from anything other than a tin cup. More importantly, Mrs. Squires kept the best-looking girls west of St. Louis, for all those pleasure-seeking men with enough money to burn a wet elephant.

Up till then, I'd never had dealings with the lady or any of her employees. But I heard she could be a handful f you crossed her. City law enforcement types complained about her inclination toward violence, and a short article in all the local papers once noted her skill with the big end of a pool cue. Seems an inebriated drummer named Homer Locksley took it in mind to beat the hell out of a soiled dove Mrs. Squires harbored some affection for. When Lilly Belle finished with the girl's belligerent customer, he had a cracked skull, broken arm, and shattered shins.

Giggling rumors flew around town that she'd waited till Homer passed out, sewed him into a sheet, sat next to the bed till he woke up, then beat the unmerciful hell out of him. Made a mental note to be careful should I ever encounter the lady. Figured anyone that calculating deserved a wide berth.

Unfortunately, Fort Smith still had dirt streets. Always seemed dustier than a sulfurous hell. City fathers hired a new town marshal named Augustus Starr. Man actually took his job seriously. He kept the main thoroughfares clean, the drunks locked up, and even enforced the often forgotten ordinance against letting pigs run loose or sleep in the alleyways. Stepped on some toes in the process, but all us boys in Parker's corps of lawdogs liked the man for his dedication to a fairly thankless job.

By that point, my wife and I owned the general mercantile store Jennings Reed left Elizabeth when he passed, and the hardware store two doors south of it. Enterprising woman that she was, Elizabeth even bought the place right next door to Reed's on the north side and moved her women's clothing operation into it.

As more and more females showed up in town and tamed their individual choices from the rowdy masses of unshaven, hairy-legged men available, they insisted on having access to the finest fashions Mrs. Tilden could import from back east and the Continent.

Eventually Elizabeth went into the wedding apparel business—on a small scale of course. But overnight the thing turned into a huge undertaking, and we'd talked a time or two about buying a bakery over on Rogers Avenue, just to provide the cakes and such for all the nuptials she now arranged and catered.

With all that, the Elk Horn Bank and fifteen or twenty rent houses spread around town, Elizabeth Reed Tilden had managed to make us a fairly wealthy family. Seemed to me everything the woman put her hands on turned into money. Hell, I didn't *have* to chase bandits and killers, but other than Elizabeth, the Midas touch never came anywhere close to where I was standing. Besides, I didn't really know how to do anything else. Dogging the trails of bloodletters and bad men just came naturally.

Tied Gunpowder to the hitch rail outside Reed's and strolled into the store with Caesar dogging my heels. The gigantic mottled yellow beast ambled to a corner near a barrel full of ax handles, sniffed out his favorite spot, pawed at the rough plank floorboards till he'd got enough of his scent planted, then flopped down and stretched out, like he expected to get paid to sleep all day.

Attractive, pint-sized clerk, with fiery red hair and a button nose, named Millie Mae Greenwood, spotted me from behind the counter and flashed a winner of a smile my direction. "Morning, Marshal Tilden."

"Morning, Millie. Mrs. Tilden in today?"

She did an abbreviated curtsey, batted long dark eyelashes at me and said, "Yes, sir. And I'm certain she'll be thrilled to see you." She leaned slightly forward, pointed along the shiny countertop toward the office, and motioned me that direction.

Elizabeth's involvement in a pile of store ledgers kept her from noticing me leaning against her open door for about a minute. With one hand, she rocked a cradle that sat beside the chair Jennings Reed left his daughter, and made notes in her accounting books with the other. Every once in a while, she would stop the scribbling, glance down at the baby, smile, then go back to her work.

Swear, when Elizabeth spotted me from the corner of her eye, you'd have thought Hayden Tilden was the only man living in Arkansas or the Indian Nations. Trust me on this folks, there's just nothing like a good woman's unbridled love to make a man feel like he doesn't really need any of the worldly things most people pine for— at least not as long as she's staring into his eyes. Then again, having that same woman kiss you till it feels like your socks are going to burst into flames don't hurt much either.

When our lips finally parted I said, "Well, Mrs. Tilden, I do declare. Does your vagabond husband know you're given to kissing strangers like that?"

She nuzzled against my neck and whispered, "Well, when I see him across from me in the bed tonight, I'll ask him." Smoky, sensual, and almost a growl, her voice stoked a blaze in me she couldn't have put down with a fire hose and a hundred-pound block of ice. She dug playfully at my ribs with a stiff thumb, bit my earlobe, and pulled back slightly. Good God, but the woman held the key to every aching cell of my shuddering being.

Pulled her as close to me as I could. Kissed the top of her head. "Too bad we don't have a bed right here

in this office. Given as how we own the place, don't see
why we couldn't put one in here."

She leaned back and laughed—a deep, free, lusty
sound I loved hearing from across the bed in the dark—
and said, "You are such a bad boy. A bed in my office?
What would the clerks think? Sweet mother of pearl,
one of our noisy after-dark sessions and the Baptist Ladies' Committee for a Decent Society would run us out
of town on a rail. That's why I built our house out on
the bluff, between here and Van Buren. Figured we
could make all the noise we wanted." She chucked me
under the chin and pecked me on the lips again.

"So that's why we're living so far out of town. Been
wondering about that ever since we moved."

She took my hand and pulled me toward her desk.
"Come see your son, Marshal Tilden."

Clear blue eyes set in a chubby smiling face gazed
up at me from the crib. Elizabeth reached down, fetched
him up, and handed the boy to me. Cradled him in the
crook of my right arm and tickled his chin with my
finger. His whole body twitched and jerked at the same
time with the pleasure of it, and the grin got bigger.

"You know what I think, Mrs. Tilden? Think it's time
for Thomas Jefferson Tilden to take his first ride on a
horse with his father. Maybe just to the end of Towson
and back. What do you think?"

My grinning wife grabbed me by the arm and quickly
guided the two of us back toward the store's plate glass
door. "It's a grand idea, Mr. Tilden. He needs some time
outside, and I need a little break." Could tell, from the
sound of her voice, she wanted us both gone for a few
minutes—and an hour or so would be even better.
Couldn't blame her much. The boy was just another re-

sponsibility on top of all the others that had piled up on her.

Passed Caesar as I headed for the door. "We're going for a ride, big dog. You want to tag along?"

His monstrous head came off the floor for about a second and a half as he assessed whether anything real important was about to take place, or the possibility something to eat might be involved. Guess when he decided his help wasn't needed—and no food was in evidence—he snorted, flopped back down on the rough-cut boards, and fell asleep by the time Tommy and I reached the hitch rail.

Elizabeth stood just outside the doorway of Reed's Mercantile and proudly watched the two most important men in her life saddle up for a nice afternoon ride. A hand shielded her eyes from the sun, as I climbed on Gunpowder and nudged him into the seething tide-like flow of people moving south in the direction of the courthouse and cemetery. Held Tommy in front of me so he could see all he wanted, and everyone we met could see him.

Had to have been an exciting ride for the boy. He giggled, waved his arms, and pointed like he knew some of the folks we passed in the street. Wagons, animals of every kind, and scores of people contributed to the hectic patchwork of movement and noise that surged around us. A cloud of red dust drifted back and forth on the warming breezes that darted between the buildings along Towson. Nose-tingling odors of every kind imaginable wafted their way up to us. Wasn't exactly what one might refer to as an *assault* of sweat, animal waste, and human debris, but it came close. And, to be absolutely truthful, the scene and situation was considerably better than when I arrived back in '79.

We'd only gone a block or two when I spotted the lanky crane-like figure of Billy Bird as he made his agitated way toward us. Still amazed me that a man that thin could stand erect with a matched pair of those Smith and Wesson Schofield .45s strapped around his waist. Pulled Gunpowder up in the middle of the street and waited for my friend to elbow his way through the multitudes.

The skinny marshal whipped his hat off, grasped the leather lariat hanging from my saddle, and said, "Knew you'd get around to replacing me as a running buddy sooner or later, Tilden. Just didn't realize you'd settle for one this young. And, hell, he's so short on top of that. Reckon I need to find him a matched pair of these big ole pistols anytime soon?" With his free hand he pushed the walnut butt of one of the weapons forward.

"Well, we might want to wait till I can get him used to a horse, Billy. Once I've got him riding like a Comanche, we can start some training in the use of firearms and knives. You can do the pistols, and we'll get Old Bear and that meat cleaver he calls a bowie for the blade work."

Billy grinned big, slapped his hat back on his head, and started looking serious. "Carlton says you boys are going down to Phantom Hill after the Crooke brothers. Wondered if you might want some company. Things have been some slow for me lately. Had to testify at four trials. Been sitting around the courthouse for almost a month. Judge Parker can put on a court case faster than a six-legged jackrabbit, but trials still take time. Besides, my pocketbook ain't seen any greenback money in so long a time, a family of field mice have taken up residence there."

He stopped a second, waited for the proper dramatic

effect, and rubbed his rump. "Think. those cane-bottomed chairs in the marshal's office have put a callous on my behind the size of a Shetland pony's saddle. I need to get out of town before this slab of skin on my backside grows so big it takes on a life of its own and has to be amputated. Gonna look pretty bad for a deputy U.S. marshal to have most of his ass cut off."

Tried to stifle a snicker as Tommy squirmed in my arms and patted the saddle horn. "Well, Billy, you're gonna have to stop catching folks so evil they'd steal a widow woman's only milk cow. Heard you and Bix even had the almighty gall to jerk Axel Grubbs up short and drag his sorry behind in to face Judge Parker's wrath."

"You know, Tilden, tried for years to be nice to ole Axel. Knew him from his whiskey-running days. He'd been in jail at least a dozen times for introducing. Never took him for a murderer though—leastways, not till he snuffed Nathan Wyatt over in the Cherokee Nation a few miles west of Maysville. Way me and Bix figured it, Axel caught Nathan asleep beside the road not far from George Woman Killer's farm. Nathan was on his way to Siloam Springs and must've camped there for the night. Had a sack full of cash in his war bag he intended to use to buy some cows. Family claimed it was in the neighborhood of five hundred dollars.

"Anyhow, Axel shot the old man a couple of times. Robbed him. Dumped the body in the bar ditch. Nathan's wife identified the remains by its clothing. When we caught up with Axel, he was drunker than an English lord and sittin' on several new, untapped kegs of rotgut gator sweat. Found most of the money in his vest pocket. Old man Wyatt's saddle and boots were under his bed. Axel never was very smart, but I guess all that hooc made him stupid and careless. Only took a few days for Judge Parker to sentence him to hang for the robbery and killing."

Billy paused, his head dropped, and he started laughing. "Axel said he didn't think he could stand being in jail long enough for the hanging to take place, Hayden. Judge Parker told him to do the best he could. Axel whined around as how he got headaches from being inside too long. Honest to God, Judge leaned over from the bench and handed him two papers of patent headache powders and told him to take one a month till his time came."

He jerked his hat off and whacked me on my leg. Had himself a real belly slapper of a laugh. Tommy clapped his hands and laughed, too. Billy said, "Swear, Hayden, sometimes ole Judge Parker's a real caution, if you pay attention and listen to what he says. Think I'm gonna stop by Axel's cell every couple of weeks and see if he's had to take them powders yet."

"I'll be in town for at least a day or two, Billy. Looks like you'll have to rub a little more fuzz off the marshal's chairs till I can get my own business with the court settled up. If you still want to go after the Crooke brothers with us, just check with Carlton. We can all head for the Nations together, soon as everything here in Fort Smith shakes out."

"You've got a deal, my friend." He smacked me on the leg again, stuffed the hat on his head, pulled at the brim, and winked. Then, he disappeared into the masses of people, animals, carts, wagons, and noise that flowed around us like lava rushing down the side of a volcano.

Took Tommy out to Belle Point. We rode right to the edge of the bluff. Held him up so he could see where ~e Arkansas and Poteau Rivers joined. Boy acted like it tickled him to death. Wonderful thing about babies, least bit of stimulation and their entire bodies react. Whole shebang gets to jerking and quivering. Touch one of 'em on the little toe and they'll laugh and flop for a whole minute. Same kind of reaction occurs with the newest things they can see. He must have liked what I showed him. Tommy couldn't hold still and giggled and pointed across the Arkansas to the Nations. Seemed almost like he knew what he was doing and where his father worked a dangerous job.

I pulled him close and whispered, "Asked your mother to marry me over there on that patch of grass under the big oak, son. We would come out here on Sundays, throw a picnic blanket on the ground, and do what old folks used to call sparkin'." He blinked, gurgled, and smiled. Know he didn't have any more idea what was going on than a month-old calf, but it was fun thinking he might. "Good thing I did, ole hoss. Otherwise, you wouldn't be around to see all this." He clapped his hands and drooled all over my arm.

We met Elizabeth back at the store and stayed around till she got ready to quit for the day. After the first couple of years of seeing me come and go so often, it had got to a point where my arrivals and departures seldom caused much of a stir, and rarely interfered with the operation of her various businesses anymore.

She always said, "I love you, Hayden. You and Tommy mean more to me than anything else in the world. But romance is romance, and business is business." She tended to lean pretty hard on the last part of that sentence. I had come to the conclusion her philosophical bluntness was just a living piece of the personality Jennings Reed left with his daughter when Tollman Pike put a pistol ball in the old man's brain. Understand-

ing that went a long way toward explaining why she
made me pay for anything I took out of her hardware
and mercantile operation. Didn't mind it at all. Fact is,
I not only loved but also admired the hell out of the
woman. And besides, at home, at night, after dinner, you
would never have known those words passed that beautiful girl's rosy, dew-covered lips. Good thing she built
our house way up on the hill out north of town. Damned
good thing.

Actually got lucky that time around. Managed to
stretch my stay for as long as I could. Layover even
included a Sunday. To this very day, memories of morning services with the Baptists and afternoons on my veranda, where I snoozed off the pleasures of a fried
chicken and mashed potatoes dinner, can wash over me
like a wave when those same meals are dished up at the
Rolling Hills Home for the Aged in Little Rock.

All together, when everything at the courthouse, and
at home, finally worked out, it took three days for the
whirlwind to finally suck me up and turn my head back
toward the Nations. Bucked the criminal twister for as
long as I could though, and wasted half a day in Elizabeth's office, mooning over my wife and son.

While those times at her store, amid canned goods
and accounting ledgers, provided fond memories, the
most enjoyable part of my increasingly brief Fort Smith
stopovers was the simple pleasure derived from sitting
in my own kitchen in the evening while the most beautiful woman in the world fussed over my supper at a
cast-iron stove that glowed.

I'd light myself one of those panatelas my old friend
Handsome Harry Tate favored when he was alive,
bounce the boy on my knee, inhale all the most plea-
surable aromas of baked apple pies, buttermilk biscuits,

the warmth of hearth and home, and wonder at my inability to spend more of my time in the bosom of my family. And even after the passage of so many years, my dreams still swirl and twist with the sights and sounds of days long forgotten and only brought to life in those hazy, jumbled, and sometimes confusing visions.

2

"Evil Men Seldom Rest for Long"

WHILE I DAWDLED with Elizabeth and the boy, Carlton and Billy whittled, spit, wasted time playing washers or pinochle, and champed at their bits like a pair of hot-blooded racehorses. Hadn't heard from Judge Parker or his personal bailiff, Mr. Wilton. Figured a job on my own wouldn't hurt anything, and if they wanted me, I was usually pretty easy to find.

By that point in my career, several rail lines had punched their way through most of the Nations, from the north and east. The M., K., and T. ran through Cherokee, Creek, and Choctaw country all the way from the Kansas line to Texas. Went right through Atoka, but you had to take the Arkansas Valley west from Fort Smith to make a connection. The Frisco Railroad was a damned site more convenient. It headed south out of a depot right there in Fort Smith.

Unlike me, most of the court's deputies couldn't afford to ride the rails. Getting paid was a pretty iffy proposition that usually took place about once every six months, even if our luck held. Some of the men got so desperate they had to borrow against their earnings with speculators who didn't pay but sixty cents on the dollar. It was a problem I never had to worry over. And since I'd been the reason we were slow getting out on the trip, it didn't trouble me much to spring for my spirited friends and I to load our horses on a slat-sided boxcar and make up lost time in glorious comfort all the way to Antlers.

Told Carlton, "You and Billy meet me at the Frisco Depot, and we'll ride down like some of those greenhorn English buffalo hunters out on a western lark."

"Damn glad to hear it, Hayden. Bunion on my left foot's been achin' for almost a week. They's bad weather coming. Gonna rain like pouring it out of a boot onto a flat rock. Billy will be happier'n a blind pig in a peach orchard when I tell him."

Left Carlton and strolled by Mr. Wilton's office for a courtesy visit. Sent my calling card in and waited till he could see me. Didn't take long. Fact is, my rump barely hit the leather seat of a chair in his outer waiting area when he called me in. His office was very much like Judge Parker's, only smaller. Instead of two windows, he had one. The room was large enough for a mahogany desk, several bulky bookcases, a pair of overstuffed chairs, and a couch. But Wilton kept the curtains closed, which made the room appear smaller to the casual observer.

"Most pleased to see you, Marshal Tilden. Hear you just brought Zack Queen to heel." He clapped me on the shoulder, guided me to the chesterfield just inside his office door, and sat down beside me.

"Yes. But it could have gone the other way. Could have easily killed the man. But he put on a right pitiful act after a slug from the Winchester brought him down. Took me a week to get him back. Given the severity of his wounds, he might not make it to trial anyway."

"So I understand. A doctor saw to his injuries shortly after you dropped him off. Man has the constitution of a range-crazed longhorn steer. Sawbones said Queen would live plenty long enough for Judge Parker to hang him."

"His kind of killer deserves a quick one."

Several seconds passed as he clipped the end of a fine-looking panatela with a tiny pair of silver-plated scissors, licked the cigar to moisten it, and heated it from end to end with a match. Once he got the thing going good, a heavy aroma of rum and spice filled the air.

"Would you care for one, Marshal Tilden?" He held the leather case out and shook another smoke loose for me.

"No, thank you, sir. Have my own, but will wait till later to partake."

"Do have one. You'll like it, I assure you."

Didn't want to insult the man, so I smiled, pulled his offering from the case, and slid it into my own.

He took a deep pull on the brownish-black stogie and puffed blue rings toward the ceiling. Between them, he said, "Suppose . . . you're here . . . to inquire . . . about possible new assignments."

"Yes."

He picked an errant piece of tobacco from his lip and

dropped it into a silver tray on the table near his end of the couch. "We do not have any pressing business for you at the time. Should you wish to take on other obligations, please feel free to do so. I understand Marshal Cecil might lead a party on a search for the Crooke brothers, and your friend Marshal Bird has expressed a desire to accompany him." The depth of his knowledge about our plans impressed me. He must have guessed what I was thinking. A toothy smile spread across his ebony face.

"You are well informed, sir. Marshal Cecil asked me to go with them on the trip, and I have agreed. But I wanted to clear all such efforts with your office before taking on any task that might keep me from being available for you and the judge."

"Please, go with your friends this time out, Hayden. Should anything arise, it most certainly can wait until your return. Presently, though, I am fairly confident your *unique* services are not required." He stood, held out his hand, put his free arm around my shoulders, and walked me back to the door as we shook.

"Round up the Crooke boys, Marshal Tilden. I'm sure there'll be something in the offing when you get back. Evil men seldom rest for long." His door clicked behind me as I made my way down the hall and back into the brilliant Arkansas sunshine.

Elizabeth brought Tommy down to the freight yard the morning we shoved off. They waved as the shining, gold-trimmed steam engine huffed, puffed, belched a billowing veil of black smoke, banged, clanged, slowly ground spark-slinging steel against steel, and pulled us away from the depot. Guess that was the first time my son actually saw his father head out for the wild places in search of bad people. Figured it wouldn't be his, or his mother's, last time—not by a damned sight.

Stood in the open door of our car, with Caesar by my side, and waved till my little family vanished in a cloud of locomotive smoke, coal dust, and morning mist. Stared into the grayish haze for a long time past when I could still actually see them. Those departures always hurt back when the only person I had to leave behind was Elizabeth. Tommy's tiny waving hand added to the lingering heartaches and made the whole process even tougher. But I had to go. Elizabeth understood why, and someday, I hoped, so would our beautiful son.

Bad men had done evil things. My friends and I would jerk them up by the roots and chastise them in the most severe manner. The Crooke brothers didn't know we were coming for them yet. But, when those boys finally got the news Hayden Tilden, and company, dogged their trail, a boatload of quaking and second-guessing would get done by men I'd already sworn would live to regret their wicked deeds. Either Maledon would hang 'em or I'd kill 'em. Whichever way it fell out in the end, Mary Beth Tall Dog and her daughter would be avenged, so help me God.

When Billy showed up that morning, he looked like a raccoon that'd had the hell beat out of it. Black circles around his eyes set off an egg-sized knot right above his nose. A long, ragged, blood-encrusted slit zigzagged its way through the lump, and headed into his right eyebrow. When he pulled his hat off, the boy's entire forehead was an ugly patchwork of blue, black, and purple.

Carlton sounded amazed when he yelped, "Damn, Billy. What in the hell happened to you, son? That gal you been seeing get after you with an ax handle?"

Billy kicked around in the hay covering the floor of the railcar with the toe of his boot. His embarrassment was obvious when he finally mumbled, "Sally's a tough ole gal, but she ain't that tough. Honest, boys, y'all ain't gonna believe what happened when I tell it."

Carlton and I took up our most learned attitudes, sagely scratched our chins, and eyeballed him like he was an insect under a college professor's magnifying glass. Leaned toward Carlton and kind of whispered, "Well, you know, Carl, I once saw a feller who got kicked by a mule. Looked a lot like Marshal Bird afterward. Don't suppose that knot on his head is part of a hoofprint, do you?"

Carlton sounded as serious as a doctor who'd just discovered a case of diphtheria. "Nooo, Marshal Tilden, sir. It couldn't possibly be something as odd as that. We would have surely heard about any poor, injured farm animal near Fort Smith that'd broken its foot on a man's head. Hell, newspaper reporters from as far away as St. Louis and Chicago would've been in town to report a scientific oddity of such monumental significance." Carlton laughed like his joke was about the funniest thing he'd heard in years.

Billy gingerly ran his finger over the tender scab-covered spot between his eyes. Sarcastic disdain dripped from his words when he said, "Marshal Cecil, that's just so damnably funny. Eddie Foy couldn't hold a candle to your wit if the two of you ever appeared on stage together. Bet you could black up and sing "Mammy" with the best saloon performers around."

Cecil and me couldn't help ourselves. The snickering just wouldn't stop. We'd seen Billy at breakfast the day before and nothing appeared amiss. Now he looked like a team of spirited horses had stomped all the juice out of him, then dragged his bloody carcass all over Fort Smith.

Our lanky, wounded friend kept beating around the bush like he was trying his best not to get at an explanation. "Heard once some feller a lot smarter'n me said that the truth is stranger than anything a body could make up or write down. But, truth is, when I think on it much, have a hard time believing how I got this shiner myself."

Carlton snatched his hat off and ran knotted fingers through thick, reddish hair. "Well, try us out, ole son. Don't know about Hayden, but think I'd just about be willing to buy a ticket to hear this one." He punched me on the arm with his elbow. "If this tale's good enough, we could start a traveling show of some kind. Make some money on the side. Maybe get rich like ole Hayden. Can you pick a banjo or play the wire and tub, son?"

Billy snorted his disgust at being hurrahed, gazed at his boots, and mumbled into a tale he obviously didn't care to tell. "Well, yesterday morning, after breakfast with you boys, went back to my loft to take a nap 'fore I had to appear in court again. Just moved into the place about a week ago. It's on the second floor in the Widder Calder's room and board over on Garrison, three blocks from the opera house. Anyhow, woke up and realized I was running a few minutes late. Hopped my way down the staircase on the side of the building. Took the thing three steps at a time. Got all the way to the bottom and some unthinking son of a bitch had left a yard rake on the ground right in front of the last tread. Somehow me and my spurs got tangled up in the rake. I stumbled, pitched forward, flew through the air like a Civil War mortar shell, and hit the corner pillar on the widder's front porch headfirst."

Carlton eyeballed me from under the brim of his hat,

winked, and dove back in. "Ole son, you're among good friends here. You don't have to hold anything back. Do you mean to tell us that God snuck up on you and hit you in the head with a house?"

Billy slapped his leg with his hat. "Dammit, Carlton, this ain't funny. Hurts like hell." He gently ran the tip of his finger around the wound again. "Honest, boys, it didn't look too bad at first. But when I woke up this morning and checked the thing out in my mirror, thought a week-old corpse was staring back at me. Ain't seen a face this bad since the time we pulled Lonesome Edgar Steele out of the Poteau River after he'd been under water for a week." He shrugged and rubbed his neck. "Think I knocked a kink in my spine right between my shoulders. Been hurtin' and achin', something terrible."

No point passing up a chance like he gave us. Figured I might as well get my share of funning in while I could. "Well, Billy, kind of think you'd have to expect some serious aching, here or there, when you damn near get knocked into next week with a picket the size of a porch pillar. Guess it's a good thing your head's as hard as a frozen turtle's shell, or Carlton and me would probably be attending a funeral today. Course the inscription on your tombstone would be a novelty. Guess it'd have to read something like, 'Here lies William Tecumseh Bird— killed by the Widow Calder's colonial-style porch.' Damn. You were right. That would be embarrassing as hell."

Carlton's eyes kind of flipped up into the top of his head. Then he fell straight backward in the hay and rolled around laughing like something crazed you'd expect to find over in the Arkansas State Mental Hospital. Threw wads of straw in the air and giggled out, "Well, did you fight back, Billy? You didn't let that sneaky, underhanded boardinghouse get away unpunished, did you?"

For the first time, our lanky friend grinned, did his 'I'm so embarrassed I could die' act again, and said, "Damn, Carl, to tell the truth, it made me so mad—you know, the falling and all—and embarrassed me so much, guess I musta lost my mind for a second or two. Hate to admit it, boys, but I jumped up and shot hell out of the Widder Calder's corner post."

Carlton went hysterical for about five seconds. "Oh, my glorious God. You shot the Widder Calder's house?"

Billy didn't miss a beat. "Yes sir, I did. Four times."

Flabbergasted is the only word I could think of for a second or so. Put my hand on the boy's shoulder. "Four times, Billy. You shot a poor defenseless house, with no weapon of its own, four times? Where was the Widow Calder during all this madcap gunplay?"

He dug around in the hay with his toe again and kicked some of it toward our still giggling friend on the floor. "Think she was serving hot lunch to some of her other boarders, till the blastin' started. Claimed it almost scared her and the rest of 'em to death. Even threatened to call the city marshal and have me arrested for disturbing her peace. Can you picture that? Deputy U.S. Marshal Billy Bird having to appear in city court and tell the story you just heard. God Almighty, that would've been awkward as hell. People would still be talking about that when I'm as old as Judge Parker. Widder made me promise I'd pay for a new corner post and not shoot at any more of her property. Entire dance was damned embarrassing, boys, mighty damned embarrassing. Jesus, you know what it's like to get a cut on your head. Bled all over hell and yonder. Soaked my best shirt all the way to the waist. Cain't remember a single time

I've ever been so mortified in my whole life."

Carlton stuffed his hat over his mouth and yelped, "Damnedest thing I done ever heard, Billy. You're absolutely the very first feller in all my vast experience as a man hunter to wound a boardinghouse."

Well, after me and Carl finally broke down and showed the proper amount of sympathy for our wounded *compadre*, we threw our saddles in a semi-clean corner, fluffed us up a nice pile of hay, and slept most of the way down. Got mighty comfortable by the time that freight train punched into the Nations. We could have taken a seat in the caboose with the brakeman, but agreed the open air was a welcome change from being cooped up in Judge Parker's Fort Smith courthouse.

I remember Billy tenderly pulled his hat down over his eyes and muttered, "Sure beats the hell out of riding a horse. 'Specially when you've got a head on you like this 'un. Guess I should be glad that yard rake didn't fly up and jab a string of holes in my behind." Well, that one set us all to laughing again.

Caesar perked up next to me, grunted his displeasure at being awakened by the noise, nuzzled back into the hay, and was asleep faster than I could snap my fingers. Restful slumber always came hard for me. The dog's ability to drop off into dreams of cat chasing, big, meaty bones, and such, baffled and sometimes irritated me. Hated the fact that I envied him such a simple animal skill.

Think Billy came up with the business about the rake while we were running through the leading edge of a rainstorm a bit south of the San Bois Mountains. Ten-thousand-foot thunderheads blotted out the sun and for a spell it got almost dark as night.

Carlton observed as how it's always a damned site

nicer to be high and dry than wet and miserable. Couldn't argue with either assessment, but knew if the squall kept up for long we'd end up getting soaked to the bone sooner or later. Caesar thumped his tail against my leg, ran in place, and snored away.

3

"KILLED EVERY DOG WITHIN A MILE OF HERE"

SEEMED LIKE WE made stops at every bump in the rail bed to load, and unload, piles of freight or animals. And while the delays did tend to slow us a bit, the trip still went pretty fast. Got to that mud pie of a town, Antlers, around four in the afternoon. Two days quicker'n riding a horse.

Carlton had sent a telegraph message to policeman Dennis Limber Hand a day of so before we struck out. Guess Carl figured he'd be making the trip, even if he and Billy had to leave me moping around over my wife and son for another two or three days.

Soon as our boots hit the ground again, my friend pointed Limber Hand out for me. Indian lawdog rested comfortably on a thick blanket with his back against a sheltering tree that acted as a huge umbrella. Looked as though he'd picked the only dry site for miles. Soon as he spotted Carl, the short, stout officer stood and drifted over. Helped us unload our mounts, the pack animal, and all our other gear. We pushed west for Phantom Hill less than half an hour later.

Limber Hand dressed himself like a white banker. Wore a matching suit coat and vest. Stuffed his wool pants into mule-ear boots. Topped the entire outfit with a wide-brimmed felt hat crimped in a military peak. Covered a white shirt that had no collar with a large, wine-red bandanna, and pinned the silver shield of the Choctaw Light Horse Police over his heart. Carried what looked to be a brand-new stag-handled Colt pistol across his belly behind a thick, fully loaded double-row canvas cartridge belt. Man looked more than capable to me.

He and my yeller bear of a dog took an instant liking to one another. Caesar ambled up to our new friend and wagged all over. You'd a thought they'd been trail mates for years. The Choctaw lawman scratched behind the big animal's ears, then leaned down and whispered something. The two of them were inseparable friends from that moment on.

Have to admit it was the first time I'd had any close dealings with a full-blood Indian who barbered his hair and dressed himself like a man who might loan me money. But over the years, I'd managed to suppress my prejudices and preconceptions, and accept those men on an individual basis like anyone else. Most of the fellers who made up the Indian police force tended to be hard workers, dogged on the trail, and deadly accurate in the most blistering gunfights. Just the kind of companions I wanted with me when a lethal barrage of .44-caliber whistlers started cutting holes around my ears.

We let Dennis lead the way, but didn't get far before

dark came down like thunder. Spent what could have been a miserable night out on the trail. Rain fell like lead shot bouncing off the bottom of a number ten washtub. Pitchforks of electric-blue lightning spiked their way to the ground, and often lit the tired faces of companions anxious for some relief.

Rigged up a good-sized lean-to shelter. Personally thought a fire was out of the question, but our guide managed to get one started. My guess was we couldn't have found a dry twig within fifty miles, but he did it. And after about thirty minutes or so, things got right toasty. By the time sunlight forced the stars into their disappearing act, the downpour drizzled to a stop, and we'd even dried out a mite.

Hour or so after the sun came up we made it to Phantom Hill. There wasn't much in the tick-riddled dump most folks today would even recognize as a town of any consequence. German fellow, Gerhard Spicer, owned what passed for a general mercantile. Like most whites, he'd tiptoed into the area illegally, but married a Choctaw gal named Esther Little Moon soon as possible so he could stay around and open a business. His wife's striking good looks, and never-met-a-stranger friendliness, probably helped his business more than he had brains enough to realize.

Their *store* might have had a grand total of a dozen items available for purchase. Mostly they sold flour, dried beans, tobacco, and smoked bacon. Carlton bought some of the meat and a dozen cackle berries for our next breakfast. He had a hell of a time keeping those eggs intact, but somehow managed.

A combination livery stable and smithy's venture was run by a friend of Limber Hand's. Every exposed inch of Jackson Lame Elk's skin glistened black from a forge he kept going day and night.

One-room church building, of uncertain denominational affiliation, sported a painted cross over the front door and looked like the only structure that'd had some real effort put into the construction of its whitewashed walls. Circuit preacher probably passed through about once every six weeks. In the meantime, folks starved for a spiritual balm for their immortal souls made do with services conducted by self-appointed deacons. While adequate, such amateur ministers were usually a poor substitute for the real, honest-to-God, Bible-thumping, hellfire, and brimstone thing.

The only other undertaking of any substance was a lowdown makeshift lean-to affair used for gambling, whoring, and other such less-than-Christian social endeavors. Heard Lame Elk tell Dennis it had once served as the tack room for a horse corral. According to the talkative blacksmith, the Crooke brothers sold bust-head whiskey from a clearing behind the joint and, generally, caused about as much trouble as they could when the spirits they sold, and from which they liberally partook, burned up enough brain matter to overcome their better judgment.

Lame Elk whacked at a glistening horseshoe and sent sparks flying in all directions like fireflies mounted on Chinese rockets. Carefully inspected the results of his efforts and said, "Them boys get nuttier'n a gunny sack full of pecan shells when they've been drinkin', Dennis. Year or so back, Myron went on a brain bender that didn't end till he'd killed every dog within a mile of here. Had me a three-legged mutt my son called Peanut. Liquor-crazed son of a bitch kilt poor ole Peanut, too. Don't understand it myself, but seems to me like every drunk in the Nations goes to butcherin' dogs once they get good and lubricated up. Damned hard to keep a pet round these parts."

He punched the shoe into a barrel of rainwater. Steam sputtered, hissed, and sizzled around the hot metal as he lifted it out and eyeballed the finished result. "Thought about trying to stop him myself. But when them boys is suckin' up that stump juice, you'd best step aside, or die like one of those dogs. You catch up to 'em, be especially careful of Byron. He's one crazy white man when the liquor takes hold and washes away all his self-control."

We only stopped long enough to give our horses a short breather, roll a smoke, let Carlton do his shopping, and give Limber Hand an opportunity to socialize a spell with Lame Elk. Quick as time allowed, we tipped our hats, said our thanks, and headed south and west of town about five miles to what had been the coarse home of Mary Beth Kincade Tall Dog and her recently vanished daughter.

Appeared Mary Beth's long-dead husband worked mighty hard at clearing thick stands of scrub oak and pine from the side of a low hill. But typical of the Nations, and that time and place, his squatty shack looked like it could barely stand on its own. Single rooms on either side of a dog-run porch, in the middle, comprised what most folks used to call a *shotgun* house.

Kitchen made up the room on the left, and the sleeping area occupied the area on the right. Person standing on the porch could see an outhouse sixty or so feet behind the main building. A ramshackle barn, on the west corner of the property, appeared capable of holding two or three animals.

Near as I could determine, the entire shebang had

never seen a paintbrush and wore the grayish-brown tint of rough-cut green lumber, battered and aged by weather, time, and neglect. Not one blade of grass grew in the swampy, much abused yard.

Sun darting between clearing storm clouds caused the mud to glisten like reddish-brown gemstones. All the people had been gone long enough to where there wasn't much to smell, except for a stunted crab apple tree that blossomed near the corner of the front porch. No animals in evidence. Even the chickens had abandoned their former home for the seeming safety of surrounding bushes and trees; but soon as they saw us come up, the skinny birds dropped from their leafy perches and gathered under our feet in search of food.

A tumbled-down rail fence encircled most of the property, and did almost nothing in the way of keeping anything in or out. Most prominent landmark in my memory was the heaped mound of a freshly dug grave in the family cemetery on another runty hill, slightly behind the house and about a hundred feet to the east.

Four wooden markers gave proof of the short, hard quality of life on the edge. A sheltering aged oak hovered over the forlorn cemetery like a tired angel who'd somehow got lost and accidentally found his way to that pitiful spot. Way I figured it, those graves were for Tall Dog, his recently departed wife, and perhaps a couple of infant children who didn't make it past the first few years of a cruel life that created hard men and bitter women.

Limber Hand stood on the steps of the rugged porch with his reins in one hand and whacked them against his other palm. We sat on our horses and listened to the creaking of leather as he pointed to a spot just outside the doorway of the kitchen. What he said betrayed a man who'd known the victim and harbored a deep sadness over the brutal way she passed from this life.

"Found Mary Beth outside kind of flopped over next to the kitchen door there on the porch. Not much of her clothing left. Most torn off and discarded in several places out here in the yard. Near as we could determine, the Crooke boys chased her all the way around the barn and back. Caught her on the porch, did their business. Must have decided to keep the story from being told. Shot her at least twice—once in the head. Did it right where we found her. You can still see the bloodstains, and some brain matter, on the doorjamb and threshold."

His voice cracked. He stopped for a moment and let his arms drop to his sides. "She fought 'em. I came upon a piece of cloth under her body when we picked her up. Ripped from a shirt everyone recognized as having belonged to Myron Crooke. Personally think she hid it just for me."

He pulled a hand-sized patch of brightly colored material from his pocket and offered it. "Easy to spot. Not many men around here wear a garment with that much red and yellow in it. Ole Myron loves his bib-front shirt. He's always considered himself something along the lines of a strutting peacock. Took to wearing a big white plume jammed in the band of his hat. Folks said he'd found a book and come upon the picture of a Civil War general that sported one. Others said the dumb ox drank so much and was just so stupid he'd come to believe he was a real skull-and-bones pirate. His brother, Byron, is almost an exact opposite. There's dirt enough under Byron Crooke's fingernails to raise a five-acre crop of yellow-meat watermelons. Most folks pretty much agree he's dumber than a dead armadillo, and dangerous to boot."

The Indian policeman stopped for several seconds. I thought maybe he'd said all he wanted for about a week or so. He removed his hat and mopped at misted eyes with a blue bandanna.

"I knew Mary Beth and her daughter, Precious. They led hard lives, Marshal Tilden. But they was mighty good people. We looked all over, but couldn't find the girl. Tracked the murderous scum 'bout thirty miles north and west. Decided they took Precious with them. Only God knows what they've done to her by now." His head dropped to the point where his chin rested on his chest, and I barely heard it when he mumbled, "Hate to think on it."

Carlton threw me a quick glance, stepped off his horse, and started up the steps. "Have any idea where they were headed, Dennis?"

"Yeah, reasonably sure. Those boys have friends over on the Washita, north of the Arbuckle Mountains, not far from a greasy pimple folks over that way call Boiling Springs. It's one of those no-place-else-left-to-run hide-outs that everyone out here and his brother knows about." He waved his hat in a general westerly direction and let his arm drop back against his leg like a man too tired to hold it up. "Bunch of bad folks living around that hellhole. That's why I waited on you boys. Could have been there and back twice by now, but I'd probably be deader than a cut-glass doorknob in a Texas whorehouse."

He'd brought us out to the scene of Mary Beth Tall Dog's death for a reason. So, I figured he wanted us to look around some and get a feel for what we would be dealing with. Carlton had already given everything a pretty good going over by the time I stepped down and strolled through. Caesar snuffled around from one end of the house to the other.

Exterior belied what lay inside the rustic place. Probably the cleanest home I'd ever seen, given its location and history. Looked to me as though Mrs. Tall Dog spent a good deal of her final few minutes of life in a valiant effort to keep her attackers outside, so they wouldn't disturb anything. Then again, she might have just been trying to keep them away from the daughter. You just never knew what folks would do when confronted with people who'd commit a murder of such unprovoked depravity.

In one corner of the kitchen, next to a Chief National Excelsior cast-iron stove, an enormous solid mahogany glass-front knickknack and china cabinet loomed over the entire room. Astonishing piece of furniture for a backcountry home in the Nations. Stood in front of the thing and tried to figure out how on earth they'd managed to get it out there. Had to have been one hell of a tough operation.

Collection of salt and pepper shakers decorated most of the shelves. Looked like three dozen or more of them—all kinds, shapes, and sizes. Lady of the house seemed to have held a special interest in anything fashioned like a teapot. Several different varieties of that particular type ornamented the shelf in the middle. A broken chair sat just inside the doorway next to the wall and was the only thing I could detect as having been mistreated. A thick layer of undisturbed dust had begun to collect on all the furnishings and every other flat surface available.

Bedroom was equally well kept. Limber Hand motioned around the ten-by-ten space with his hat. "Surprising thing is that those fellers didn't tear this place down to the foundation, or burn it to the ground. Guess they got themselves in something of a hurry after they'd murdered a woman loved and respected by her neighbors. Way I figure it, the Crooke boys probably got scared somebody would catch them in the bloody act. Truth is, it almost happened just that way. Friend of Mary Beth's, named Rufus Iron Ax, came on the scene a few minutes after the heartless killers' departure. He's nigh on eighty years old, and still scared to death of the white man's treachery. Had me out here about three hours later."

Gonna have to admit here, I never got used to crimes committed against women or children. Never could stomach gratuitous slaughter, no matter who got butchered. Shame of it was that such indignities were almost commonplace where the only law for most folks resided in a family Bible they likely couldn't even read. Badge-wearing men, like me, were located so far away in Fort Smith, that the most barbaric kind of ill treatment often went unpunished.

But even our heavily armed, law-bringing presence didn't always deter unlawful acts. Criminal activity of the most heinous kind often got done within a few miles of deputized posses, out on missions to bring stability to the region. After almost half a century's consideration of the matter, I've come to the conclusion that if evil men want to do something, they will, and nothing can stop them—short of a large caliber bullet in the brain box.

In the case of Mary Beth Tall Dog and her daughter, we found ourselves confronted with a combination of brutal crimes. It surpassed all understanding, for me, that men could sink so low as to rob, grossly mistreat, and murder females who generally didn't have any more chance than hummingbirds in a cyclone of defending themselves against such slop-swilling swine. But it happened. Truth of it back during those years was that almost half of all the murders we had to spend time investigating revolved around the final results of a mindless attack on some poor unsuspecting woman. Seemed as though brutal rapes almost always ended with equally horrific killings.

Billy stopped his ramblings just long enough to gaze through the china cabinet's milky glass at what appeared to be small portraits of each family member. Several traveling photographers were known to frequent the Nations and eke out a meager living making such miniature likenesses. Most claimed to have learned their trade during the Civil War, and harbored an unwavering affection for our red brothers, along with a robust fury over—what they deemed—the American Indian's gross maltreatment by our government. As a consequence, you could usually find it easier to produce the photograph of a member of the Five Civilized Tribes as find one of any of the whites in the area.

Billy flipped the latch on the cabinet door, pulled Precious Tall Dog's rendering from amid the maze of teapot saltshakers and stared at it for several seconds. He ran a tentative finger around the frame as though trying to seek out some small portion of the girl's spirit that might possibly still reside there.

"This looks like the talent of Stanford B. Anderson. Seen a lot of his stuff. He likes to put a bit of color in his photos. Fine feller. From Pennsylvania, I believe. Told me pictures he took at Gettysburg had the power to bring grown men to tears. Showed me some of his war prints once. They were brutally compelling images. Personally, I like his portraits best, though. Seems to have a real talent for young women. Ever met him, Hayden?"

"No, Billy, don't think I have."

"Does beautiful work. You should have him make a portrait of Elizabeth. Won't find anyone who'll do it better. From the stories we've heard about Precious Tall Dog, I'd say ole Stanford ought to get first prize for this one. Mighty pretty girl," he said and offered the likeness to me. Boy darted a glance at Limber Hand and, under his breath, whispered, "Makes a man's blood boil to think what those low-down, scurvy sons of bitches may have done to her."

The gilt-edged wooden frame contained a striking vision of what the photographer had seen. Got the impression Billy might have fallen just a bit in love with Precious Tall Dog's wistful copy. Black eyes dominated a striking face outlined with braids wrapped in ribbons that had been hand tinted in red by the artist. Entire package got tied up with the moon-shaped smile, typical of those too innocent to have any idea what the future might hold at the hands of men who had no earthly concept of beauty, or how it should be respected and cared for.

Longer those black eyes stared back at me from that haunting reflection, the more I realized how much she looked like my sister Rachael. And how Saginaw Bob's bunch of killers stole that beautiful girl's life, an act that sent me on a mission to rid the world of their shadows— an undertaking I'd come to believe hadn't yet ended for me. Such thoughts and beliefs still plagued my nightly dreams, even though I'd personally sent all the men responsible for Rachael's death to scorching, blackened perdition. And even though the sun was full up and blazing by then, hellish chills chased one another up and down my back, like waves lapping at the edge of a wind-tossed lake.

Billy fidgeted, slapped a leg with his hat, and snapped, "Let's get after these animals. Running dogs like this don't need to be loose on poor, unsuspecting folk who'll surely suffer if they just happen to meet up with 'em. Quicker we put a muzzle on these bastards, or kill the hell out of 'em, the better off everyone's gonna be." We couldn't have known how prophetic his notions would prove.

Carlton leaned against the door frame and tapped the butt of his pistol with a nervous finger. Had absolutely no doubt both my friends itched for a chance to erase the soggy damp from their bones and rectify the horrible wrong done over the threshold of Mary Beth Kincade Tall Dog's kitchen door. Best way they could think of to accomplish such a needed and desirable end involved sweaty horses, gun smoke, and shackled men presented to Judge Parker for executioner Maledon's brand of twisted rope retribution. Course, if the Crooke brothers chose not to go along with that idea, shoveling coal in Beelzebub's furnaces was just as good. Knowing Billy Bird the way I did, he'd have been more than glad to accommodate them at the first opportunity. Realized that I'd have to keep a close eye on my posse. Carlton and Billy in the same party bespoke a combination of fire and action anyone would find hard to control, when the chips finally fell.

While we saddled up, Limber Hand made one more pass through the empty house and respectfully, almost tenderly, latched the door to each empty room. As though at military attention, he stood on the porch and snugged his hat down on his head. That was the first time I noticed he had a habit of holding it by the brim with the fingers of both hands and kind of lowering it over his hair like a crown being mounted on the head of a king.

"Marshals, the Crooke brothers killed a fine woman, and stole her daughter—Christian woman known by neighbors for miles around for her kindness. Think it's time we drop a loop on the Crookes and see to it they get hung," he said.

Carlton grinned at our new friend. "Sounds good, Dennis. But you're gonna have to keep an eye on Marshal Billy Bird when we find 'em. This ole boy's been known to shoot first and leave everything else to God. You ever see him whip out those Schofields, you'd best hunt something large, thick, and heavy to hide behind. Hell's bells, I've even heard rumors of shots fired at helpless Fort Smith boardinghouses."

Billy let out an embarrassed giggle, pulled his hat down over his face, then pushed it to the back of his head, spun his horse around in a tight, chicken-scattering circle, and headed for the gate. Limber Hand jumped from the porch to his line-backed buckskin mare and expertly kicked past Billy and into the lead.

I hung back for a few moments and gazed at the spot where Mary Beth Tall Dog met her end. Needed the memory of it indelibly burned into an easily available spot in my brain. When we caught up with the Crooke boys, I didn't want any doubt in my mind why they were gonna have to die. Blood on that door frame erased any hesitation I might have harbored for men I'd yet to meet.

In a matter of hours, we'd skirted the southern edges of Atoka, crossed the Clear Boggy north of Tishomingo, and made it into the rolling, long grass and sweet-smelling pine covered foothills of the Arbuckle Mountains. By nightfall, we'd covered most of the ground our

Indian guide had in his original run almost a week earlier.

Remember stopping for a moment to share a smoke with Billy. Pupils of the man's eyes had drawn up like birdshot. Knew it would be hard to keep him under control when we caught them murdering bastards. The Crooke boys didn't know it yet, but death dogged their trail. A blind man could have sensed it oozing off Carlton. I could see it plain as day in Billy Bird's eyes, and felt it sharpening its claws in the darkest corners of my heart.

4

"YOU'LL BE A CANE-CARRYING CRIPPLE"

BACK WHEN CARLTON J. Cecil still romped and stomped at the Rolling Hills Home for the Aged—and the womanly virtue of nurses and volunteer helpers hung in the balance—we used to spend a lot of time with our feline friend General Black Jack Pershing out on the sunporch studying over a raggedy-assed auto club road map of Arkansas and Oklahoma.

Cecil had surreptitiously *appropriated* the thing from an old man named Norman Krebs, who'd lived in Guthrie and claimed to have taken part in the great land rush of 1889. Norman passed away not too long after Carlton pilfered his map. Can't remember exactly what killed the old man—probably little more than the relentless advance of age and just enough family neglect to push him over the edge. Kind of thing happened on a pathetically regular basis at Rolling Hills. Don't think Norman died as a result of Carl's thievery though, because he was pretty much gone when his anxious-to-get-rid-of-a-living-problem family dumped him on Nurse Wildbank and took a hike. Carlton never admitted to larceny in the deal. He always said he'd merely "impounded" Norman's property, because the ancient codger was already dead and couldn't use it anymore, or anyhow.

Ole Norman's wrinkled-up, dog-eared highway chart brought back memories, fond and otherwise, and showed us former gunmen and killers how much things had changed over the years. In those bygone times of almost forgotten yesteryears, we chased folks like the Crooke brothers all over hell and gone, and you could have traveled for a week and not seen anything that came close to resembling a real town. Should you go there now, you'll find some kind of settlement and acres of people within spitting distance of just about anywhere you can stand.

If my ramshackle memory still serves, there's a village called Mill Creek in the north central region of what used to be the Chickasaw Nation. Not much out in that part of the country back when Billy, Carlton, Dennis Limber Hand, and I chased after the Crooke boys, though. Just a few farms here and there. Horse and cow operations tended to be rare. Livestock cost more money than most of those poor folks could muster.

Life had been harder than usual on the Five Civilized Tribes ever since Mr. Lincoln's war. Slave ownership wasn't uncommon prior to the *unpleasantness*, and many of those Indians had sided with the South. Forgiveness from the triumphant Northern winners, and their oppressive Reconstruction carpetbagger progeny, took its sweet time arriving. A vengeful Yankee government declared *all* those exiled Indian folks had allied themselves with the Confederacy, and unceremoniously forced them to sell off their western lands for as little as fifteen cents an acre.

Decimated remnants of the pitiful, beaten, smaller plains tribes got forced into those areas. Arapaho, Wichita, Caddo, Cheyenne, Pawnee, and Comanche peoples found themselves trying to scratch a living out of some mighty sorry acreage and living in conditions that were deplorable beyond imagining. Hard to believe any place could be worse than what the Chickasaws ended up with, but most of it was.

Anyhow, my posse managed to get to a spot just north of where Mill Creek is today, and we were still headed dead on for the Washita. Limber Hand scouted the trail a goodly piece in front of the rest of us. Billy, Carlton, and I stalked along at our leisure and tried to pick up on anything we thought he might have missed, which proved to be damned little. Moved at a pretty good clip, considering the rugged terrain, and had just topped a ragged piece of sawtooth rock when we came around a bend in the trail and discovered Dennis waiting for us. Nothing about his appearance gave any indication of what he'd found in a small canyon on the other side of that jagged ridge.

Pulled to a foot-stamping, gravel-pawing halt. The animals snorted and shook their heads while we gathered as close around Limber Hand as we could. Like a man trying to talk from underneath a pile of pine logs, he said, "Horrible things waiting below, Marshal Tilden. Horrible things."

Carlton snatched at the reins to steady his mount, Booger. When the big sorrel finally settled some, he patted the animal's neck, dropped the reins, and fished tobacco and papers for a smoke from his vest pocket. "Horrible? What the hell does that mean, Dennis? Don't see how it could get much worse than the death you described for Mary Beth Tall Dog."

As Cecil said his piece, I noticed a look of weary tiredness had developed around the edges of our Choctaw guide's eyes. Kind of thing that descends on a body when he begins to feel as though he's seen too much and has realized the end is nowhere in sight.

"You're gonna have to go down and look this one over for yourself, my friends. No way to give you a proper description. Even after years of eastern education, words fail me." He turned the buckskin and started back down the rugged path ahead of us, without saying another word.

Carlton threw me a quizzical look, shrugged, and pushed out in front of Billy and me. As Billy passed he muttered, "Damn. Great way to finish off the day, ain't it? Have to go look at something *horrible*. Never cared for that word *horrible*, Hayden. Usually means I'm gonna have to puke my spurs up by the time it's all over and done."

My skinny friend remained the fastest and most deadly companion with pistols I'd ever seen when confronted by evil men. But he still managed a level of feelings for innocent lives taken before their time that easily rivaled those of any teenage girl caught in the throes of heart-rending romance.

Limber Hand could have been a prophet on the order of the Old Testament's Jeremiah. He had described what waited for us below perfectly, but like the Judeans of old, I don't think any of us really believed the scene could be as bad as he indicated. Truth of it was, what lurked in the shadows at the end of our rugged trek shocked us all right to the soles of our boots.

I'd done gone and got myself all hopped up for the big push on the Brotherhood of Blood, when a waiter, dressed in a shiny black suit, silently cruised up behind A. Maxwell and whispered something in his ear. Vought made a give-it-to-me motion with his fingers, and a gaudy-looking white phone trimmed in gold appeared like a rabbit out of a magician's hat.

He said, "Hayden, please hold your thought. We have a project working at a ranch over in the San Fernando Valley, and one of my assistant directors is on the horn. Forgive the intrusion, but it's a call I must take."

For about the next minute, our movie mogul friend almost burned up a notepad with fevered jottings. Never said another word to whoever did all the talking on the other end of the line. Then, just all of a sudden like, he stopped writing and hung up. Took a kind of thoughtful pose for about a minute, waved for the waiter, and went through the whole whispering routine again. Our server did another snappy bow, scooped up the phone, and disappeared behind one of the palm trees in the corner.

Max looked worried, as he glanced around the table, and said, "Much to my embarrassment, Hayden, we've had an emergency on my set in the valley. Our presence is required for the rest of the afternoon. I've instructed Maurice to make reservations for lunch tomorrow afternoon at the Brown Derby. Alfonso will drive you. Please excuse the inconvenience." He motioned to his staff and said, "Ladies and gentlemen, I'll meet you on the set, as quickly as you can all get there."

The Hollywood types jumped up like Texas jackrabbits with their tails on fire, and hit the door running. All of them except a lady named Victoria Janes. She took her long-legged, slim-hipped time. Girl kinda moseyed over, leaned down, caressed my wrinkled, liver-spotted hand and said, "You're quite something, Hayden Tilden. Think I could listen to you tell your stories all night long. Can't wait till we meet again at the Brown Derby, where you can continue with the Brotherhood of Blood."

And then, as God is my witness, she winked and kissed me on the cheek. Nurse Heddy McDonald got a look on her face like she was gonna slap my newly acquired Hollywood girlfriend till all the curl came out of her hair.

Being practical people who'd survived the Great Depression, Frank, Heddy, and I decided it would be mighty wasteful to walk away from a table with that much food on it. So we ate all we could hold and had the waiters bring along what was left to our room by the pool when we finally retired. I'd been sitting next the window, enjoying the view for about an hour, when the driver, Alfonso de Blanco Cardiñas, strolled up and tapped on the door.

He removed his shiny-brimmed cap, stuck his head inside, and said, "Buenos dias, Señor Tilden."

"Come on in, Alfonso."

"Señor Vought has instructed me to drive your party to the Brown Derby restaurant tomorrow at eleven."

"Yeah. He and his traveling band of toadies got called away on some kind of emergency out in Fernando's valley. Said he'd meet us for lunch at that hat shop you mentioned."

A broad grin spread across his face. "Are you enjoying your trip, señor? Is California to your liking?"

"Oh, I guess so. There is one thing I haven't seen so far that I'd rather not miss if I can keep from it."

"And what is that, sir?"

"The ocean. Haven't seen the ocean. Sure would like to get a gander at one, before I saddle up and ride off into the sunset. Hate to meet my friend Carlton J. Cecil on the other side and have to admit I made it all the way to the West Coast and didn't manage to see it before I checked out."

"The Pacific is but a short distance from here, Señor Tilden. I am at your complete command and would be honored to drive you there. Where are Nurse McDonald and Mr. Lightfoot?"

"Franklin J. Junior took a cab over to a dry goods outfit in Beverly Hills named Bullock's. Said he had to get his wife something to carry back to Arkansas, or she'd probably skin him alive. Nurse Heddy staked an early claim on a lounge chair by the pool." I pointed out the window. "She's over in the corner. Claimed she can keep an eye on me from over there, but I think the feller she's been talking with might have diverted her attention just a bit with all those muscles and corn-colored hair."

"*Es muy bueno, mi amigo.* I will ask her if she would like to go to Santa Monica."

Heddy bounced into the room all fired up and ready to hit the road. Girl absolutely glowed. Don't know whether her demeanor came from the relentless California sunshine, or the undivided attention oozing off her blond swimming-pool god with all the muscles.

She threw a little skirt of a thing over her bathing suit, tied a scarf on her head, and said, "Let's go to the beach, Hayden."

I loved the girl's spunk, and the fact that she looked fantastic didn't hurt a whole lot. Let me tell you something, there's just nothing like the stir an old fart causes when he's seen in the company of a beautiful young woman. Heddy turned a lot of heads as we strolled through the hotel lobby. Alfonso had the Cadillac waiting.

Pulled away from the hotel and turned onto a wide, tree-lined avenue. Over his shoulder Alfonso said, "This is Sunset Boulevard, Señor Tilden. She runs all the way from here to the ocean. Sit back and enjoy the ride." Nurse Heddy and I did exactly what he recommended.

The spacious, twisting street climbed steadily for a good piece, before it started a steady slope toward the ocean. Beautiful Spanish style homes on either side all along the way—kinds of places you'll only see out on the West Coast. Lots of whorehouse-pink stucco and red roofs.

Took about twenty minutes to hit the ridge on the mountains. Pulled off the road into a spot that Alfonso called a scenic turnout. "There, Señor Tilden—the Pacific Ocean." He said it with amazing pride, and motioned across the universe like all that water belonged to him.

Guess if I'd been paying attention, I could have seen it myself. But being able to stand on a rugged, windswept cliff and come to the sudden realization that the cool breezes on my ancient face rose up from the blue at my feet was almost overwhelming.

Smoky gray hills like undulating waves ran for several miles and vanished into a steel blue line that ran from one end of the world to the other. Billowing white clouds rolled toward us and shattered the dwindling sunlight into thousands of glasslike shafts that cut into the sea.

"Your ocean's beautiful, Alfonso. Just beautiful."

"Si, señor. Ella es muy bonita."

Ten minutes later, we hit a stretch of highway that

ran due south along Alfonso's ocean. Needless to say, landlocked country folk like Heddy and I were beyond impressed. She gazed at the rolling sand beach and crashing waves, held my hand, and tears streamed down her cheeks when she turned to me and said, "Hayden, how can a country girl from the rude hills of Arkansas ever thank you for this?"

Couldn't think of a thing to say. Truth of it was, if it hadn't been for Franklin J. Lightfoot's stories, neither of us would've been there to see something that magnificent.

Just as the sun started to dip low on the horizon, Alfonso pulled our land boat under an arching multi-colored sign that read Santa Monica Pier. The well-worn wooden wharf looked every bit of a quarter mile long. We left the car in a spot reserved for VIP types.

Alfonso and Heddy helped me cane my way to the end of the rolling jetty and into an enormous, noisy, bustling restaurant. In pretty short order, our Mexican guide managed to get us seated in a booth that allowed for a stunning view through the glass windows behind the bar and directly at the ocean.

Awestruck, beautiful Heddy, and her ancient ward, watched as a molten-iron sun bled into a sizzling ocean on the other side of the waking world. I had observed the same glorious event thousands of times out in the Nations. Watched, and wondered, at the mystery of it all my life. Carlton J. Cecil used to have what bordered on religious experiences over the coming of morning and the end of the day. But as my old friend might have said, there just ain't nothing like being witness to the thing from a whole new perspective to really get your undivided attention.

Whole scene caught me by surprise. Reminded me,

in no uncertain terms, just how close the end of my time to behold such a wonderment really was. Remember thinking, damn, while it was a pleasure to share the affair with someone who appreciated it as much as Heddy, it sure would have been nice if Elizabeth could have seen it with me. For the first time, realized how much I regretted never getting the chance to show her an ocean when she was alive. Course she'd seen the one in New York, and I hadn't. Made my shortcomings a bit easier to take.

Bartender brought us some potent drinks in tall, thin glasses. Laughed like a loon when he walked away. Stuff tasted amazingly like Rolling Hill's iced tea. But, oh my God, when I finished that sneaky beaker of liquid dynamite, I felt better than I had since my seventieth birthday. Even got the urge to dance for a minute or two. Had to give up on that one though. Was confronted with a very simple fact—desire and doing are two entirely different things when you're damn near ninety years old.

Our stolen afternoon by the Pacific finally came to an unwanted end. On the way back to the car, we had to pass through a somewhat poorly lit area in the parking lot. A skinny hairball dressed in ragged clothing, and covered in stinky filth, jumped from behind a trash barrel and waved a butcher's knife around in the air like a cavalry saber. Scared the hell out of Heddy, and that made me madder than a Mexican hornet with its stinger out.

Grubby bastard yelped, "Gimme yer goddamn money, or I'm gonna kill all three of yah."

Heddy fumbled with her purse and started crying. Alfonso feverishly went to digging in his pockets. Guess I didn't move fast enough to suit the thief.

"You too, grandpa. Get your retirement wad out here where I can see it."

Switched the cane over to my weak side and reached into my waistband. Pulled the silver-plated, bone-handled Colt pocket pistol out and leveled it up at his innards. Dumb goober's eyes got the size of the Cadillac's hubcaps, but he tried to bluff his way out.

Pointed at me with the knife and said, "What the hell you think you're gonna do with that thing, old man?"

I rolled the pistol over to where he had to stare right into the muzzle and said, "I'm gonna count to three. You'll very gingerly put that knife on the ground by the time I'm finished, or my first shot will blow most of your right kneecap into tiny jagged pieces." Grinned real big and added, "It's a damned painful wound, sonny. Chances are you'll be a cane-carrying cripple, like me, for the rest of your natural life."

Would-be robber got a serious case of religion. Held his arms out and tried to squat. "Sweet Jesus. Wait a minute, old-timer. Careful now. Knife's a-going on the ground. Knife's a-going on the ground. Ease up. Ease up." He placed the meat carver at his feet, and slowly stood again with his hands in the air.

"Kick it into the gutter," I said.

Not sure Heddy or Alfonso had taken a breath during the whole exchange. It got so quiet I could hear the ocean breaking under the pier back behind us. Our failed thief frowned and toed the knife about six feet into a concrete trench filled with running water.

"Now come over here, sonny. I've got something important to tell you, and want to be certain you hear me."

Let him get mighty close before I said, "Stop right there." He wobbled to a halt and glanced down at his feet as if embarrassed by what had just transpired. "Look up here at me." When he tilted his head, I whipped my walking stick around and caught him just above the bridge of his nose with that gigantic gold elephant's head. His eyes crossed and rolled back into their sockets. He dropped to his knees and kind of flopped over on his side like a rotten tree. Twitched a bit, and finally went as stiff as a frozen carp.

For about five seconds, it got quieter than the bottom of a grave. Then Heddy whispered, "What have you done, Hayden? Is he dead, do you think? Oh, sweet weeping Jesus. You didn't kill him, did you?"

"No, darlin'. He's not dead. Just put him to sleep for a spell. He'll come around in a couple of minutes. By then, we'll be long gone." Walked over, eyeballed our fallen highwayman a mite, and added, "And when he wakes up, it'll be a damned long time before he tries to rob anyone my age again. Gonna have a nice-sized knot with a split in the middle of it for about two weeks. Should leave a scar that'll stay with him for a stretch. Look kinda like my friend Billy Bird did after he rammed the porch pillar with his noggin." Took the cane and punched the unconscious bandit in the ribs. "Damned lucky Carlton J. Cecil ain't here, you thieving son of a bitch. Instead of a minor headache, and bruised opinion of yourself, you'd be dead. Old bastard carried a .45 under that leg warmer of his. Makes a lot bigger hole than this miniature pop gun."

Turned around and caught Heddy and Alfonso looking at me like I'd lost my mind. Figured we'd better get things moving so I said, "Well, let's go home. No point standing around here."

Started for the car and Alfonso said, "Don't you think we should call the police, Señor Tilden?"

"No need, Alfonso. Think our outlaw amigo has

learned his lesson. Besides, if you call the local constabulary, they'll probably try to take my gun away from me. Wouldn't want to be forced into shooting a Los Angeles cop, now would we?"

"Oh, no. No sir. Wouldn't want to do that."

Well, once we got rolling again, and put the episode behind us, my new trail mates loosened up considerably. Lots of nervous laughter and retelling of the whole incident as we made our way back to Beverly Hills. By the time Alfonso pulled up in the hotel driveway again, it was just another fun-filled California memory.

Had to swear them to secrecy though. Didn't want Lightfoot or Max to find out about our Santa Monica adventures and figured my accomplices in assault and battery didn't want to spend any time talking with representatives of the local police. Probably wouldn't have looked good if a story came out in the L.A. papers about an eighty-nine-year-old retirement home resident from Arkansas beating the hell out of a much beloved California bandit. Heddy and Alfonso agreed wholeheartedly.

All three of us were pretty high on ourselves when we finally got back to our room. Frank J. Lightfoot Jr. acted all upset and put out with us. Said we should have talked it over with him first. Course, reminding him that he'd gone on a shopping trip for his wife and couldn't be consulted didn't do much good. Guess the fact that Heddy and I'd also partook of a few more tall, icy drinks with little umbrellas in them didn't sit too well with him either. Not that we were drunk, mind you. But I'll admit, we did feel mighty good and pretty full of ourselves. Leastways, till the next morning.

5

"LEFT WHAT YOU SEE THERE IN THE TREES"

WOKE TO BLAZING California sunshine—another perfect day. Except this one was accompanied by a skull buster of a hangover. Swore right then and there I wouldn't be sucking down any more fruit-flavored, sugary drinks. Hell, I'd known for more'n sixty years, if you want to be safe, you stick to straight-up bonded bourbon over a few ice cubes—if you can get the ice. Neat, if you can't. Couldn't even begin to look breakfast in the eye.

Alfonso brought me one of those bloodred tomato drinks. He sat the concoction on the table and whispered, "Little hair of the dog that bit you, amigo." Man knew from whence he spoke. Heavily peppered pick-me-up helped a bunch.

By the time we arrived at the restaurant for lunch, I

was about ready to eat the seat covers in the car. Couldn't believe my tired old eyes. Entrance to the building was shaped like a derby hat and painted brown. Soon as we got inside, a snooty twerp in a black suit hustled us over to a secluded corner.

His highness, Mr. Snooty Twerp, and a pair of white-jacketed helpers, seated us at what the Snoot sneeringly said was "Mr. A. Maxwell Vought's favorite table." Then he did a lot of finger snapping and, quicker than you can hiccup, I was holding a bill of fare that looked like volume E from a set of Judge Parker's encyclopedias. Evidently, the menus were just for show. Max had already ordered for us. He, his whole traveling company, and the food arrived at almost the same instant.

Vought bustled in under a cloud of cigar smoke and said, "Please forgive our tardiness, Miss McDonald, gentlemen. We had another emergency this morning. A small, but irritating, fire had to be put out on a project in Palm Springs." He waved his party to their individual seats. That's when I noticed that a good-looking woman named Lisette Tully wasn't among the faithful.

As she seated herself Victoria Janes said, "Lisette will be a few minutes late, Hayden. She asked that I extend her apologies."

Actually couldn't have cared less if our potential director, John Robert Chastain, or his assistant, Millard Ellingsworthy, showed up or not. Hell, if Chastain had burst into flame on a Beverly Hills corner that morning, it wouldn't have mattered to me. As long as Lisette Tully and Victoria Janes were in attendance, I knew we'd once again have a good meeting. Good for an old fart like me, at least.

Hated that the girl hadn't been able to be there, but my regrets didn't last long. She came running up and grabbed the seat beside Victoria. Popped her napkin open and said, "Sorry, everyone." Girl looked like a million dollars in newly minted hundreds.

Max acted the part of genial host again, even let everyone get finished with his meal, before he moved the conversation back to a discussion of the previous day's tale of murder and insanity. He said, "Think I can speak for everyone on my side of the table when I say you caused quite a stir with your opening account of the Brotherhood of Blood, Hayden. In spite of our problems on the set, my associates have literally buzzed with excitement all afternoon." He smiled and nodded my direction.

"Mighty kind of you, Max. I'm pleased you and your staff decided to attend today's quilting bee so you could hear the rest of my story. At least I hope that's why you all came."

Everybody, except Ellingsworthy, smiled, nodded, and looked thrilled and expectant over the prospect of me continuing with my murderous tale. He slumped in his chair, with his head propped up by a lazy hand, and assumed the expression of a man about to be bored in the ground like an Oklahoma oil-drilling auger. I reached over and caressed the head of my walking stick. Wondered if maybe I should give him a rap on the noggin, too. Just to get his attention, you know. Decided against it. Two lumpy heads in as many days might draw unwanted attention my direction.

Pulled the cane across my lap and studied the details of the gold elephant's head. Memories of the day ole Boots shot me in the leg brought a grimace. Said, "Well, if those drinks we had out on the beach yesterday didn't burn up too many of my ancient brain cells and I remember correctly, we left off somewhere around the time our Choctaw guide, Dennis Limber Hand, informed Billy Bird, Carlton, and me that he'd found something 'horrible' at the bottom of a small canyon. Went a pretty good ways toward upsetting Billy before we got down there. But, damn, friends, there's upset and there's upset. No way to imagine what a man means when he's as secretive as Limber Hand acted. But good God Almighty, we found out pretty damned quick he wasn't one to sugarcoat much. Leastways not that morning."

I urged Gunpowder into the single-file line behind Billy. We brought up the rear of a slow-moving parade. Probably took the whole traveling doo-dah show nigh on to half an hour to make the trek all the way to the bottom. Heavy cover of pine, oak, and walnut trees closed in on a rock-littered zigzagged trail that disappeared into an insignificant valley, steeped in ominous mist-shrouded fog.

Greenery grew so tall and thick it choked off most of the light. But errant shafts of the sun's glare still sliced their way earthward and managed to cut through the dense overgrowth, like a magician's collection of polished steel swords shoved through slots in the mysterious black box where his beautiful assistant lay quivering, waiting for certain death.

Honest to God, it felt like we rode off into a well. A cramped and forbidding place, where we already knew shocking things awaited our arrival. For the hundredth time, my closest friends and I made our tentative way into a land of danger filled uncertainty and the open jaws of a grinning Death. His hooded figure always seemed to shuffle just ahead—a chilling apparition that beckoned to us with a crooked, skeletal finger from the darkness and haze.

By and by, Dennis brought our funereal-like procession to a halt, and we spread out in an irregular line beside him. At first, none of us could see exactly what he'd found. Carlton pinched the bridge of his nose and rubbed at his face with the back of a sweaty hand in an effort to help uncooperative eyes cut through a gloominess even deeper than any we'd penetrated so far. Billy removed his hat, stood in the stirrups, and squinted into the shadowy clearing like a wizened old man whose vision no longer served him well.

Eventually, the grisly scene floated out of the vapor like a bloated body rising from the bottom of a lake that glided to the dark, watery surface, and popped into focus right before our unbelieving eyes. Below me, near a rock large enough for a man to stand on, a low, rumbling growl clawed its way from Caesar's chest, and the hair on his thick mottled back and enormous head stood straight out.

Dennis snatched his hat off and stuffed it onto the horn of his saddle. He leaned backward and placed a stabilizing hand on the buckskin's rump as though to move as far away from the grisly sight as possible.

"Near as I can make out," he said, "our good friends, Myron and Byron Crooke, probably came upon these folks by the merest of accidents. Stole what they wanted. Did as they pleased, and left what you see there in the trees."

In the trees—phrase sounded innocent enough. But, oh my God, what those boys left *in the trees* was enough to make the burn-blistered and puss-covered damned of hell's deepest circle cringe in horrified disbelief.

Dennis pointed at the jumbled campsite. "Looks to me like this party of pilgrims got caught napping. Seems the typical case of a family of unfortunates who lacked the slightest understanding of our little piece of hell, and not a single inkling of the dangers around them. Maybe they came down here because it seemed safer as a campsite. We'll probably never know. Hard to tell who the poor folks might have been, or why they got caught up short the way they did. Whatever their reasons for being out here like this, they probably shouldn't have been, and fate put them in the wrong place at the absolute worst possible time."

Clothing, cooking utensils, personal belongings of various sorts, and pieces of harness lay scattered on the ground around the moldering remains of a small wagon. A broken trunk disgorged its contents in ever-widening circles of discarded garments and other intimate family items. A bolt of shockingly red material flowed over the cart's tailgate and ran about the camp like a river of blood. A ragged piece of singed tarpaulin, strung between two trees, drooped over the residue left by several charred bedrolls.

The entire area had been set ablaze—including what appeared to be the corpses of a pair of men hung, upside down, from one of the tree limbs used to anchor the tarp. Useless arms dropped straight down from the bodies as though pulled loose at the shoulder. Their mangled fingertips dragged the ground. Deep scratch marks decorated the blackened earth around piles of greasy innards as though the charred dead had violently clawed at the unreachable earth in an effort to get away from the flames or knives used to torture them.

Limber Hand shook his head as if still in doubt of what his weary eyes showed him. "Didn't look these folks over real close before I came back for you boys, but think they were gutted just prior to being torched."

The coal-colored carcasses twisted slowly from the

burned wagon's creaking trace chains used to hoist them onto the tree limb. One body's intestines hung half in and half out of the remains and covered the overwhelming agony visited upon the departed soul's tortured face. Lifted my eyes to heaven, in hopes some relief could be found there, and through the dense foliage saw puffy white clouds twist above us against a cheerfully blue sky.

Billy groaned, between one of the periods when he clenched his teeth so loud it sounded like a beaver gnawing his way through a green cottonwood sapling. He turned toward me and whispered, "Damn, damn, damn. Coulda gone the rest of my natural life and not had to look at a sight like this, Hayden."

Barely heard Carlton when he said, "Sweet weeping Jesus, thought I'd seen it all, boys. You chase bad men around the Nations long enough, and you can bear witness to just about every imaginable kind of cruelty and slaughter. Seen things that'd curl the hair on an Arkansas razorback hog. But this 'un takes the cake. Good God Almighty, this 'un takes the goddamned cake."

The creak and moan of our saddles added to the overall ghostlike eeriness and dreadfulness of the gory scene. For several minutes the silence crept up and down my spine like ice water in the winter.

Chastain started chewing on A. Maxwell's ear, and it began to look to me like he was determined to whisper Max slap to death. Vought nodded about twenty-five times, and finally held up a restraining hand to try and stop the onslaught. Several of the other attendees squirmed in their seats. Millard Ellingsworthy drained one of those things they called *screwdrivers* like it was a glass of that genuine mountain valley water folks over at Hot Springs still sell to unsuspecting Yankees from places like Pennsylvania.

Max said, "My colleague here is very concerned about what you've just described, Hayden. He has rightly noted we could never put such a scene in a film. Blood-spattered gore, innards hanging from bodies, people knifed, gutted, and burned on top of that is a bit much for the tender sensibilities of 1949's movie audiences. And that doesn't even make passing mention of the profanity."

Lightfoot reached over and put his hand on my arm again. Heddy had me by the other one. Guess they were afraid I just might come off my chair and try to beat the blue-eyed hell out of those snot-nosed idiots.

"Maxwell," I testily noted, "it's just a story, son. You can do with it as you please, for the right amount of money. But it's a long way from being finished. You want to hear the rest of it or not? Or, maybe I should be asking Mr. Chastain if he can stand to listen to what I've got to say. You boys expressed something more than a passing interest in hearing this tale the other day. Came here just to hear me tell it. Got nothing for you but the unvarnished truth, fellers. If hell's too hot for you, maybe I should stop."

Victoria Janes pushed her glass toward a hovering waiter who poured another bloody red drink for her. "I'd like Mr. Tilden to continue. I find him and his story quite fascinating. What do you think, Lisette?"

The Tully woman had been virtually mute, up to that point. Whatever her opinions, she'd kept them to herself and had slumped back in her chair. She'd crossed her hands in her lap like she could care less what was going on. But she sat up, shot a withering glare at Chastain, and said, "Go on, Mr. Tilden. This is probably the best thing I've heard in months of sorting through sorry books and worse screenplays in an attempt to find something worthwhile to make into a film. While it could be true our patrons might have some difficulty with such murder and mayhem, we should be able to adapt your story by making the proper adjustments to such scenes. I find all this fascinating, and can't wait to know how it comes out. Not often someone like me gets to hear the real, true, and actual story from a man of your experience and background. Please, do go on."

She settled back into her seat and kept staring at Chastain as though she'd thrown down the gauntlet and couldn't wait for him to pick it up. That's when I realized, while the women across the table might have been introduced as this or that assistant, the two of them could well be more powerful than I first realized—perhaps the money, or at least some of it, behind the throne.

"Be happy to, Miss Tully." I smiled, winked, and nodded her direction. She smiled back. All the encouragement an old yarn spinner like me ever needed.

For an agonizingly long time we sat in our saddles, stunned by the sights before us, and tried to make sense of the horrifying spectacle. No way to do it. The crackling corpses bumped against each other in a light breeze. Friction showered bits of blackened clothing and flesh in every direction. Ash-covered tableau extended thirty feet into the trees around those charred carcasses and created a scene so alien for the living as to make the brain and heart reel in revulsion.

Surprised that Carlton was the one who finally came back to reality and started moving the rest of us toward making some sense of the gory mess. Seemed like all the air left his body when he said, "How long ago do you reckon this happened, Dennis?"

Limber Hand sat up in his saddle and slowly placed the hat back on his head. "Oh, not more than two or three days. There are some indications the killers took their time. Must have been having fun. Tell you the truth, Carlton, think the Crooke boys have gone completely, and totally, mad—only way to explain something so ghastly. Whatever they're drinking must have burned their pea-sized brains completely up. Men I knew wouldn't do something like this. Personally, can't imagine anyone capable of committing acts of such barbarism. On occasion, I've found it necessary to hang one, or two, evildoers myself, but never felt the urge to go this far. Know some of my red brothers have done such things in the past, but this is the first I could personally bear witness to."

Billy said, "You certain it was the Crooke boys, Dennis?" The question popped out like a challenge.

"Pretty certain, Billy."

"No, you don't understand. We gotta be a lot more than just 'pretty certain' on this one. Up till now, figured we might be able to take these ole boys back to Fort Smith, 'less they just made it a point to fight it out. Now, looks like we'll have to kill them for damned sure. They ain't gonna let us take them back to hang. Men who'd slaughter anyone in a fashion this grisly won't go easy. You can bet the farm on it."

Carlton nodded. Figured I might as well toss in my two cents' worth. "Don't know about the rest of you boys, but men responsible for something like this need to meet God as soon as we can send them to him. Heartless sons of bitches don't need to breath the same air these good people did."

Billy slapped his pistol-filled holster with an open palm. Carlton snapped, "Damned right. If it comes to a vote, let's kill them first, and ask questions later. You know like, maybe after we've buried them."

In the end, we stopped jawing around, bit the big, nasty bullet, climbed down, and did what we could toward investigating the scene. Took as much in the way of proper care of those poor desecrated corpses as we could, given our limited circumstances. Wrapped each of them in a piece of the remaining tarp. Damned revolting business getting those folks off that bloody limb. Turned out one of the murdered pilgrims was a woman. Being burned up like she was made it hard to tell till we got her down.

Billy spent a lot of time in the bushes during the grave digging. Leaned on one of the shovels we found near the wagon and heaved up the bacon and eggs Carlton bought in Phantom Hill. Dennis agonized over the dead woman till we all assured him it couldn't be the body of Precious Tall Dog. Man had tears in his eyes when he finally determined, on his own, that the female we'd found was considerably older than his friend's daughter.

Once my puking trail mate finally got control of himself long enough he said, "Do you have something from Mr. Shakespeare you could read over these poor wretches, Hayden? You know, just a short passage as fittin' as what you done for Travis Teel, out there on the Muddy Boggy when Jug Dudley's bunch cut him down. No one should go in the ground after being treated like this and not have good words read over 'em. May not have a preacher out here, but these were decent people, good family stock, and I think it'd be right sorry of us not to offer up some inspirational words on their behalf."

Couldn't argue with reasoning like that. For certain, no preacher was about to do it for them. I said, "Don't know if there's anything can *fit* something as god-awful as this, Billy. But I'll try."

Pulled Elizabeth's volume of the Bard's work from my saddlebags and found a few selected lines I hoped might help those unfortunate folks into the hereafter. My friends removed their hats and gathered around some of the saddest graves ever dug. Read some passages from *Henry IV,* underlined just because I liked the sound of them.

"O sleep! O gentle sleep! Nature's soft nurse, how have I frighted thee, that thou no more wilt weigh my eyelids down and steep my senses in forgetfulness. O God! That one might read the book of fate. Death, as the Psalmist saith, is certain to all; all shall die. We see which way the stream of time doth run, and are enforc'd from our most quiet sphere by the rough torrent of occasion." Then I paraphrased the last bit, motioned at the clod-covered mounds and finished with, "Their cares are now all ended."

Carlton slapped his hat on his head and snapped, "Damned right. And the men that did murder on these poor, defenseless people ain't gonna have too many cares to worry over themselves, soon's I catch up with 'em."

Once we got to digging in the remains of the wagon, the slain couple's sad story started to emerge. Carlton found flame-scorched letters addressed to a Mr. and Mrs. Homer Richland from near Gainesville, Texas, that brought everything into sad, sharp focus.

He read one short, telling missive as the rest of us continued sifting through the wreckage. Cleared his throat and popped the cheap paper between his fingers as though to get our undivided attention. "Writer says, 'Dear Brother, Have for some time now been very ill. Cannot seem to recover from an unyielding fever visited upon me over the month past after the bay mare stumbled and fell on me. My poor luck and eventual fate has reminded me of our unfortunate father who passed when °lightning killed he and Ole Badger as they plowed the back forty in Texas.

'The farm has descended into a state of disrepair even more frightful than you would remember from your last visit. I feel compelled to seek your aid, Homer, as I do not expect to live much longer. My son, Samuel One Eye—now nine years of age, educated in agency schools, and capable—will meet you in Wetumka and bring us together should you find it in your heart to make the trip. The boy has wanted a red shirt for a number of years now. If you could bring some cloth for one, it would make a fine gift for his approaching birthday.

'Please come quick, Homer, as less of my life remains with the passing of each tortured moment. Should I no longer be here when you arrive, if God in his infinite wisdom has seen fit to call me to him, please take the boy home with you to Texas. His mother, having preceded me to glory by more than a year, agreed it would be best for Samuel given our degraded circumstances. Kiss your children for me and assure them their uncle loved them. Yours in faith, your brother, Felix.' " He refolded those carefully penned pages and slid them back into their damaged cover.

Billy flicked mud and ashes from a sky-blue, cut-crystal perfume bottle. "Sounds like we've got an orphan over at Wetumka waiting on family that ain't never gonna arrive. Boy's gonna get mighty lonesome, and unless one of us goes for him, he'll never know what happened."

Carlton wrapped the stack of letters in a piece of un-damaged red bandanna, and pushed them into his saddle-bags. "I'll take care of it when we've finished with this dance." No one asked what he meant. Didn't have to. We all knew he'd do what he'd said.

We couldn't bring ourselves to camp anywhere near the scene of that monstrous massacre. Billy professed an uncommon fear of ghosts and apparitions he felt certain would appear once the sun went down.

"Trust me on this one, Hayden. Spirits of these poor unfortunates ain't gonna rest easy. Bet they'll be out and about before the last light of day disappears." He fidg-eted and slapped his reins against his palm. Could tell he wanted to be away from the eerie place as quickly as possible. First time I'd noticed that about Billy.

Carlton strolled up and said, "Don't believe in haints myself, but do respect Billy Bird's feelings on this mat-ter. Ever seen any moonlight shades or beckonin' ghosts for real and actual, Billy?"

"No, but by God that don't mean they ain't here."

"True enough. Guess they might be hidin' behind some of them trees over yonder, or maybe under the burnt-out wagon. Perhaps 'neath that piece of flame-scorched tarp." Carlton elbowed me and smiled.

Billy didn't take the jibes well. "To hell with you, Carl. This ain't a damned bit funny, far as I'm con-cerned."

We assured him nothing but our scent would be left around the area when dark came. He grudgingly ac-cepted the situation and went back to work. After we'd scratched around in just about everything not destroyed by uncommon wickedness, we pushed on through that valley of unspeakable horror and dropped our bedrolls under a nice stand of sweet-smelling pines on the other side.

6

"Hayden Even Read Shakespeare Over 'Em"

HUNGER HAD ALL of us in its viselike grip, but Carlton was the only one who could bring himself to eat anything. He started a fire and baked soda biscuits in his Dutch oven. Bacon sizzled in the inverted lid and sent its salty aroma directly to each of our grumbling bellies. Cooked coffee drifted on the evening breeze and assaulted our noses. We stared at him in shocked disapproval as he shoved the crisp meat and bread into his mouth like a starved tomcat. Then, he flushed it all down with a scalding cup of his private formula, first-rate belly wash.

"What?" Crumbs dribbled from parched lips, as he wiped his mouth with the back of a dirty hand.

"Damn, Carl, how can you eat like that after what we just saw and had to do?" Billy asked.

" 'Cause I'm hungry for crying out loud. Ain't had nothing in my achin' gut since early this morning. Hellfire, Billy my boy, my belly's been chewing on my pistol belt now for almost four hours. Had begun to think it'd bite the cantle off my saddle." He winked, grinned, and said, "You boys don't want any of these biscuits, that's fine by me."

Billy shook his head. "That ain't the point, Carl. The point is, how can you eat after what we just saw and had to do? For Christ's sake, you helped dig the graves for some of the most mistreated dead folk I've ever laid eyes on. Not sure crispy corpses and soda biscuits go together all that well."

Cecil broke another roll open and, in the manner of a waiter in a New Orleans restaurant, daintily laid bacon strips across it. Held the feast with his pinky fingers stuck out and gnawed off a big chunk. Took his time chewing and re-chewing every morsel. When the final scrap disappeared, he sucked the ends of each individual finger on both hands and smacked his lips.

"Um-um-um, boys that was good. Can't help the dead ones any more than we've already done. Hayden even read Shakespeare over 'em." He nodded my direction and said, "Hope when I go out you can read some of those beautiful words over me, Tilden."

"Be glad to do it for you, Carlton. But, I'd be willing to bet you'll outlive all of us. Anybody as ugly and hard to get along with as you always seems to live forever. Sons of bitches don't ever manage to die. And killing one of you is harder than blowing a smoke ring in a whiskey bottle."

Carl grinned and Billy sniggered. Guess my small attempt at jocularity, however minor, helped push the sharp edges of what we'd just been forced to do a bit farther into the outer reaches of our collective memories. Course, no matter how effective my gesture might have been, it only stalled off the mind's relentless return to that ugly place for a short time. Darkness would bring sleep, and sleep would bring dreams. Kind of dreams a wise man would look forward to with a natural degree of nervousness and trepidation. Figured it might be a good idea to get everyone talking—perhaps take our minds off the horrors we'd encountered in the valley. Threw my bedroll next to Limber Hand's. Could tell he still hadn't recovered very well from the afternoon's painful discoveries.

Rested my head against my saddle and pulled a doubled-up blanket over tired, aching legs. Turned to our newest trail mate and said, "Carlton tells me you studied in the agency schools, traveled some back east, and read a little law."

He gazed into our flickering fire, sipped on a cup of Carlton's potent coffee, and wiped his lips. "Even held class for a while at Choctaw schools in Tuskahoma and Atoka."

"You were a teacher?" Don't know why, but the fact that he'd done such a thing astonished me. Guess the shock crept into my question.

"Yes. You sound surprised, Marshal Tilden."

He'd caught me, and I got defensive. "Well, not surprised so much as . . . well . . . you know . . . ah-h-h. Aw hell, Dennis, you're right. It does come as something of a shock. I mean, how'd you manage to get from a profession as noble and inspiring as teaching young people to chasing lowlife men like the Crooke brothers?"

Billy and Carlton arranged their separate nests and listened in on the exchange as he said, "My father came to the Nations with the original group of Choctaw people relocated from Mississippi. He farmed some good bottomland over near Wetumka. My brothers and I were on the way to growing up wild as wolves, and ignorant as dead stumps, when a group of Presbyterian ladies from New Haven, Connecticut, showed up and took over the management of the local Choctaw school that'd been in operation since back in '40. They even let women and girls attend—bit of a shocker those days. Our entire family had a seat on a bench next to my mother. Kind of like our own personal pew in the church. We all got started together. Everyone, but me, fell away as time went on. I just couldn't seem to get enough of books. Went through those good ladies' entire program of courses in six years. Graduated at the age of fourteen." He pulled a lung of tobacco smoke from the much-abused corncob pipe he favored. "Started teaching soon as I had a diploma in hand."

Billy flipped pebbles into the fire and said, "Back home in Columbia, Mississippi, it took me six years to do the second, third, and fourth grades. Two years each. Hell, I was damned proud of finishing as quick as I did. But my inability at book learnin' put me behind everyone my age for the whole dance."

Carlton shook tobacco onto paper and said, "Didn't care for the experience, huh, Billy?

"Not much. Had a teacher named Ephiginia Boggs. Woman was uglier than a mud house. Had a set of buckteeth big enough to eat a corncob through the cracks in a picket fence. Boys used to call her Beaver Boggs behind her back. Most spiteful woman who ever drew breath. Think she actually liked jerkin' my pants down and beatin' the bejabbers out of me anytime she got a chance. Had a hatred for men and boys that bordered on the biblical. Hell, I got to thinking Miss Boggs believed

William Tecumseh Bird was personally responsible for original sin, the fall of man, and the Exodus from Egypt. Woman could whack a body on the head with a ruler faster'n minnows can swim a water dipper."

Carlton chuckled, savoring the warm smoke that curled into his nose. "Come on, Reverend Billy. Get the spirit here and tell us how you really feel."

"Will, by God. Gave up on the entire shebang in January of the year I turned fourteen. Miss Boggs had just thumped my ass for slip sliding on the ice. Can you believe it? Blistered my butt for sliding on the damned ice. That one was the straw that broke the well-known camel's back. You understand? Don't you, boys?"

Carlton's amusement deepened. "Oh, good God, yes. Understand completely. Sliding on the ice. A black-hearted damnable sin. Remember it from my days in Sunday school. Eleventh commandment or something, wasn't it?"

Didn't slow Billy down a bit. "Jumped up in her class one day and said, 'Good-bye to you, Miss Boggs. There is no love of children in your withered fist of a heart.' Then ran like hell. Figured if I had to get my living from book learnin', starvation looked like a pretty fair prospect. Pa beat the snot out of me for quittin', but he'd done the same when a shirt-tailed boy himself. Then, one day, found I had a talent. Guns. Took my degree in lead not long after my sixteenth birthday." He pointed at the fire with his finger and made the motions of shooting a pistol.

Carlton sniggered, "You're a self-taught genius with a revolver, Marshal Bird. Ain't no doubt about it. Am surprised you had no tenderness in your own heart for schoolin' though." He put his hands behind his head and gazed at the stars that fought for viewing with the sparks from our logs. I could tell he was about to go on a cow-chip-throwing rip, and he didn't disappoint me.

"Personally, I graduated at the head of my class in all the courses of study offered. My teachers bragged on me constantly. Told everyone in Jonesboro, Arkansas, that Carlton J. Cecil was the smartest little son of a bitch they'd ever had the privilege of educatin'." Darting flames from the campfire lit a crooked smile that never left his face while he told that windy whizzer.

Tried to help him out all I could. "And a good-looking kid on top of that, I'll bet."

We all laughed, and a sly grin finally crept its way across Limber Hand's deeply lined face. "One of the Presbyterian ladies, at the agency school, had a brother that occupied a place of some importance at Yale University. Managed to get me accepted. Hadn't been for her efforts, my continuing instruction would have ended in the Choctaw Agency's clapboard building at the age of sixteen. Don't know exactly how she pulled it all off, but I spent three years in New Haven."

He stopped. Seemed lost in the past for a moment. Tapped the pipe stem against his teeth and said, "Got a first-rate education and wasn't far from finishing up, when word came that a drunk named Quincy Bobwhite murdered my father over a horse. Seems Quincy bought the animal, but never bothered to pay for it. That led to words, which led to an altercation, and the fight naturally ended in a killing. Came home and went to work for the light horse police. Caught ole Quincy out on the Canadian near McAlester. Hung him myself. Strung him up to a hickory nut tree next to Blackfish Creek. Threw out a line and caught a mess of perch while I waited for him to stop twitching."

Carlton spit a piece of wayward tobacco from his

smoke into the fire. "That's one thing I do envy you light horse boys. You can deal out your own brand of individual justice when you catch them bad ones. Seen some of your *compadres*, over in Atoka, tie Willy Little Britches to a tree and beat the unmerciful hell out of him for stealin' his neighbor's chickens, then cookin' 'em up and eatin' 'em. Deputy U.S. marshal was to do anything comparable, we'd be up to our boot tops in lawyers."

"Yeah," Billy said. "That's why I like it when the bastards resist. Means I can kill the hell out of them. Now and again, even if they don't resist, I can arrange it so they do." He slapped his pistols and laughed.

At least the conversation had moved away from our afternoon's dose of horror, so I tried to keep it going. "You got any idea where the Crooke boys were headed from here, Dennis?"

He pulled at the pipe and gazed into the night sky. "Plenty of places to stop along their way to the Washita. About four hours' ride, from here, Cyrus Barking Dog has an illegal dram shop operation going in a tent. He moves around a lot, but I know where his setup is these days. Man's been snatched up for introducing illegal spirits all over the Nations at least a dozen times. Don't do any good. Pays his fines and just goes right back to it."

Went on a fishing expedition just to see how far he might be willing to go. "Maybe you should try something like the whip used on Willy Little Britches."

"Oh, we've gotten pretty serious with him in the past. Burned his whole outfit to the ground, twice, since I took up the badge. That's why he started operating out of a tent. Said it was easier, and cheaper, to replace a chunk of canvas if we took a notion to put the match to his place again. I'd be willing to bet the Crooke boys stopped in for a little visit before they went on their way. Replenish their dwindling supply of skull popper, you know. May want to talk to Cyrus for a minute or two, tomorrow. Got to be careful though. Some real hard cases hang out around his joint."

We kicked that piece of information around for a bit, and decided Dennis knew exactly what he was talking about. Conversation drifted all over the map after that. Kind of talk men do when they're trying to get comfortable with one another. Billy told a bald-faced yarn about how his drunken father strapped the thirteen-year-old boy's ass for stealing watermelons from a neighbor. His tale started a whole new round of bluff and bluster related to growing up, getting in trouble, and having your old man blister your bottom with his razor strap. Those childhood reminiscences of coming up wild eventually gave way to more intimate details of our individual lives.

And then, out of the clear blue, Limber Hand shocked the hell out of all three of us when he quietly said, "I have a personal stake in finding Precious Tall Dog, boys. She's my daughter." Well, his stunning off-the-cuff declaration went a mighty long way to explaining how he'd acted at the Tall Dog farm. His final words barely died away and it immediately got so quiet you could hear hard breathing from the moths that flitted around our fire. Crickets even stopped fiddling for a about a minute.

"Her mother and I spent the summer together on one of my visits from back east. She married Tall Dog about three months after I had to go back to Connecticut. Didn't know she was with child. She kept the truth to herself, till some years later. I've never told anyone, until tonight. Guess you boys can understand, now, why this whole thing is so upsetting to me."

Billy and Carlton both looked my direction like they expected something in the way of a sympathetic pronouncement on the level of Victorian poetry to come spilling out of my mouth. Best I could manage was, "Does the girl know, Dennis?"

His head dropped till his chin rested on his chest. He pulled the pipe out of his mouth, and what he said next came out clear as a ten-dollar St. Louis leaded windowpane. "No, but I intend to tell her—if we can find her . . ." For a few powerful seconds he faded off as though lost in thought. Then, from around the chewed stem of his pipe, he finished with, ". . . alive."

Well, that did it for the evening. Ended our rough-and-tumble, braggadocio boys-will-be-boys fest. Guess no one wanted to contribute anything else. What could we say? A new, and possibly dangerous, element had been introduced into the coming fracas. It held more than enough potential to be a contributing factor in getting any one of us killed, when we finally ran the Crooke brothers to ground and rescued Limber Hand's daughter.

The fact that each of us wanted to insure the girl's safety, and would go toe-to-toe with Satan to do it, meant there would be a fight. But now we'd have to exercise considerably more caution than we'd planned. No longer just our lives we'd be pitching on the table when the betting started, or that of a poor kidnapped girl none of us knew. Everything had taken on a dangerously different and more personal aspect. Limber Hand made it that way with his emotional revelation.

Fire finally died away, and I think most of us managed to get some fitful sleep. Attention directed at Cyrus Barking Dog gave each of us something new to consider and did wonders toward getting our minds off that afternoon's bloody work.

Everyone else snored in his blanket when the initial thoughts about the Brotherhood of Blood began to take form in my restless mind. Got to thinking, maybe it just wasn't enough for Judge Parker to have one man working for him the way I did. He'd sworn me to secrecy about our arrangement. Not even Elizabeth knew her husband was the judge's own personal assassin.

As the flames turned to embers and sparks made their way back to heaven, a notion came to me that the lawlessness in the Nations was beyond the control of an army of marshals. Maybe, I thought, half a dozen or so good men could have a far more profound impact. Especially, if word got out that when they came looking for you, your life was as worthless as having one boot and half a haircut.

Something went to working on me, and I got to thinking that no matter what we lawdogs did, evil people never changed. We could chase them down, beat the hell out of them, shoot them, throw them in foul prisons— none of it mattered. First chance out of the box, the sorry bastards went right back to doing what they'd been doing. And most of the time, they managed to rob, maim, and kill off dozens more of the pure and guiltless. Their murderous finger in the world's eye couldn't be stopped until someone literally removed their shadows from the face of this earth. Might not even be one of us badge-toting boys that rubbed them out. Usually wasn't. Most of the time the no-goods and lowlifes died at the hands of someone they called friend or family. Hell of a way to live, when you think on the problem much. Spend every waking moment loose on an innocent and unsuspecting world, just to be murdered by a *friend.* Had to be a better way. Decided I'd do a little jaw scratching over the thing. You know, think the problem over some more. Knew when the right moment arrived, God would show me the way.

In spite of my most sincere efforts, the dreams still came. They appeared to me as another graphic lesson in our collective inability to fend off the mind's ceaseless, unconscious groping for truth. But my visions that night had the feeling of prophecy—grim, frightening, determined, and remorseless. Guess maybe nightmares is a better descriptive word for what tortured my slumbers. Seemed like my head had barely touched my saddle when, out of the black depths of night, men of my acquaintance, other marshals from the army who served Parker, filed out of the darkness and passed my mossy bed, one by one.

Their shirts, vests, and breeches sported blackened, bloody holes that oozed and dripped life near my aching arm. At least three, and perhaps more—I just can't remember—stopped, called out my name, and said as clearly as ringing a brass bell on an ice-cold morning, "Good-bye, Tilden, it's been good a-knowin' you. We'll be a-waitin' when you have to give up your guitar."

Most I barely recognized, but the last to speak was none other than Bixley Conner, the very first man Judge Parker introduced me to on my arrival in Fort Smith. Bix stumbled forward, stopped at my feet, removed his hat with a blood-drenched hand, and in a voice weary from death said, "Tried our best, Hayden. Just couldn't bring it off."

From the gloomy dimness behind him, a figure draped in black from head to foot, leaped from the reddish rocky earth, grabbed my friend's collar, and jerked him into nothingness. The specter's hood fell away, and Saginaw Bob's leering, ghostly face grinned at me from the depths of an endlessly coiling hangman's knot draped around his neck.

"Thought you beat me, didn't you, Tilden?" The smirking apparition hissed. "Done told you before, boy, some of these one's are mine. Long as that scar crosses your nose and cheek, you'll never be rid of me."

Could still hear his cackling laughter ringing in my ears when I jerked myself awake and sat shivering by the fire. Cold sweat flowed along every crevice of my body. Death, of a kind I'd never known before, had been set loose on an unsuspecting world by a demon from my past. A fiend I'm certain held sway over a large part of Satan's fiery pit.

Decided not to say anything to Billy, Carlton, or Limber Hand about the visions. How could I explain them? Figured it best to just leave them be. But hidden in the deepest recesses of my tortured mind, I knew somewhere before us a horror story, unlike any imaginable, skulked in the mists, slavering, waiting, ready to pounce like Saginaw Bob's black-cloaked spirit on Bix Conner's frightened soul.

Didn't sleep much for days after that.

7

"Hell, I Ain't Got No Problem with That"

NEXT MORNING, SUN came out and burned most of those ghastly memories away. Right before Apollo's fiery orb got straight up in the sky, we topped another hill that drifted lazily down toward a stand of thick scrub and scruffy oak. Slow-moving stream, called Crooked Man's Creek, made its way through the trees and gouged out an elbow in the earth that turned sharply to the left not a hundred yards away. Lots of sweet-smelling wildflowers grew along the banks. Almost every color of God's rainbow showed up on that chiseled slice in the earth's tortured hide.

Cyrus Barking Dog had his tent as close to the water as he could get and used the gully as the back wall. Guess he'd made some improvements since Dennis's last visit. A plank partition, about four feet high, enclosed the entire canvas affair, and gave the appearance of being a kind of semipermanent structure.

Carlton said, "Looks like the man got up one morning feeling real optimistic about his future in the illegal whiskey-tradin' business." Any evidence of past burnings by the light horse police must have been cleaned up, because none of us could detect them, from where we sat.

Billy broke one of his pistols open and checked the loads. "See at least four horses down there, Hayden. Ain't gonna matter who owns them. We walk in that backcountry watering hole and it's another case of Katie bar the door. Doubt there's a son of a bitch in the bunch wouldn't kill all of us for the price of single shot of whatever kind of giggle water Barking Dog's selling."

Carlton pulled the shells from his shotgun, eyeballed each of them, and reloaded. "Marshal Billy Bird's absolutely dead-on right, boys. He just forgot to mention one very important fact concerning this sit-chi-ation. We're the law, and I'm the meanest son of a bitch within a hundred miles of here." He whipped the sawed-off barrels of the twelve-gauge upward with a loud metallic snap, and thumbed both the hammers back. "Think if there's the slightest chance the Crooke boys might be in that cow-country cantina, we need to go down and kick their butts so hard, they'll have to unbutton their long johns to tell whether it's day or night. Arrest them if'n it's possible, or shoot the hell out of them if not."

Limber Hand studied the scene like a man who wanted to spend the rest of the year in front of an easel doing an oil painting of it. "Gentlemen," he said, "most dangerous kinds of vermin you can imagine hang their hats in Barking Dog's illegal saloon. We've got to be extremely careful here, or some of us might end up dead." Man knew he didn't need to remind us of such things, but did it anyway.

Billy stepped off his mount. "Don't worry, Dennis. I won't let anything happen to you."

We tied our animals to some broken-up driftwood on the creek bank and walked the last hundred yards or so. As we legged our way in, I checked the pistols Harry Tate placed in my hands when he lay dying. Still loved the carved ivory grips. A beautiful woman's hair flowed endlessly around them and molded perfectly into my fingers. Always felt like I held Elizabeth when I pulled those weapons.

Fell in beside Billy, and remember thinking the scene reminded me of the time we'd braced Jug Dudley and his boys in Black Oak, Texas. Cocked both those big .45s, and hoped this mess worked out just as well. But, truth was, I knew when it came to gunfire, you just could never tell. One small mistake, and God would come get you so fast, you'd still be staring at the man who'd killed you and thinking you'd beat him to the draw.

Twenty-five or thirty yards from the tent's front flap I heard Limber Hand mutter, "Don't know about you boys, but I get the spine-chilling feeling there's something spooky going on here."

Water-smoothed gravel made crunching noises under our boots, and we drew to a stop long enough to give everything a better looking over, before pushing the flap back. Little breeze kicked up, and that's when the smell hit me in the face like a steaming hot towel at Yancy Thigpin's Fort Smith barbershop.

Billy yanked his bandanna over his nose and sputtered through the cloth, "Sweet merciful Jesus. Don't tell me they've left some more corpses for us."

Carl pointed to either side of the flimsy structure with

his shotgun and whispered, "Dennis, you go left. Billy, move around to the right. Check out the back. Hayden and I'll see what's happening inside." Wasn't sure I liked the way he volunteered me for our initial move past the threshold, but the deed was done and couldn't be called back.

We waited till our friends shouted that everything was clear and safe before Carl pushed the flap open again and stepped inside. Interior of the billowing canvas was barely twelve feet wide, maybe twenty feet long. Sunlight shot through the flimsy, thread-worn ceiling and lit up every gauze-shadowed detail for unsuspecting visitors. The sickening sweetness of death swept over us like a wave breaking against rocks in a tropical sea.

Stood shoulder-to-shoulder, guns at the ready, and silently eyeballed every inch of the stinking space for something to put lead in. Saloon looked like a tiny twister had buzzed through. Anything not nailed down ended up in a single pile, right in the middle of the dirt floor. Whole shebang got stacked on top of a potbellied stove. Sitting upright, in cane-backed chairs, in each corner was a dead man. Appeared they'd been propped up, posed in the hope someone would find them. A strange thought popped into my mind at the time. Seemed those poor departed goobers had been arranged to look as though they'd just taken a seat to watch as all the tables, spittoons, and other junk got pitched into a wobbly heap.

One feller had his legs crossed, a hat hung off the toe of his boot, and an unlit cigar dangled from blood-encrusted lips. Gunpowder-rimmed hole marked a spot dead center of his forehead. In the opposite corner, a second carcass had an arm flung across a bullet-riddled chest, and the only finger left on his hand was stuck up his nose. Two nearest the door appeared relatively unremarkable, except one of them had a good-sized hatchet sticking out of his skull, and the other's face had been painted black with soot and ash from the stove. Looked like he might jump up, beat a tambourine, tap dance, and sing mammy songs like he was performing in a Mississippi River paddlewheel minstrel show.

Billy pushed up beside me and said, "Good Lord Almighty." He sounded like a man so tired he couldn't hold his arms up. "These Crooke boys are some strange, widow-making sons of bitches, Tilden."

Carlton's eyes darted from corner to corner. "Yeah, and downright morbidly comical bastards when given the time and opportunity."

"Damned right," Billy snorted, "morbid, but creative."

I turned to Limber Hand and said, "You recognize any of these men, Dennis?"

He pointed to the nose picker. "That one's Cyrus Barking Dog. Think the one with the hatchet in his head is a Chickasaw horse thief named John Box. Don't know the other two. Leastways, can't tell who they are yet. Maybe when we clean 'em up a little, I'll be able to make out who they were when alive."

"You boys ever see anything like this before?" Carlton kind of threw the question in the air for whoever wanted to offer up an answer.

Billy mumbled under his breath, "Hell, I ain't never even heard the like of what we've witnessed in the last few days. What about you, Hayden?"

"Well, Billy, I thought we'd beheld the worst of it back there when we found those poor people swinging in the trees. Taken all together, does tend to make a body wonder what we're going to find next, though, don't it?" Everyone turned toward me at the same time. Eyes blinked real fast. Their faces revealed men who feared I might be right.

We spent the rest of the afternoon planting those fellers and working on the trail. Limber Hand still didn't recognize the two mystery men, even after we scrubbed them off a bit. Billy complained we were gonna have to put in for undertaker's pay when we finally made our way back to civilization. He stood in one of the rough graves, his sweat stained with specks of the red earth that rolled down his face, neck, and back.

Wiry marshal stomped the long-handled spade into the ground, threw a shovel of dirt at my feet, and grunted, "You know, Hayden, heard the court pays them grave-diggin' fools back in Fort Smith a dollar every time they bury one of Mr. Maledon's jobs. Figure Judge Parker owes me at least fifty cents each for these 'uns I buried. Didn't put them down as deep as we needed to go, but all the rocks we piled on them is just as much work in the end."

Limber Hand strolled up and pulled me to one side. "I think the Crooke boys might have picked up another hostage. Tracks still lead north for the Washita, but now there's four horses."

Didn't know exactly what to say to that, and as I tried to cover up my puzzlement by scratching my chin he added, "Could be another woman, Hayden."

"Oh, good God, Dennis. Did you know of another woman who lived around these parts?"

"No, but Barking Dog often dragged a soiled dove out for a few weeks, just to drum up a little more business. Traveling girls. You know the type. He'd go to Fort Smith, or even down into Texas, bring one back, and put her to work for a month or so. Usually about as long as any of them could stand it in such surroundings with the kind of men who patronize a place like this."

"Whole business is turning into more trouble than a tub-sized nest of yellow jackets in the outhouse, Dennis."

'Bout that time Carlton and Billy sauntered up. Carlton said, "What'd you mean by that, Hayden?"

"Well, we started out on a fairly simple-looking murder and kidnapping. So far, in addition to Mary Beth Tall Dog, we've found six more bodies. People done away with in absolutely horrible, and in the instance of these ole boys, insane ways. Hell, Carl, I'm to the point of wondering just what, in the big wide world of moonstruck lunacy, we're gonna find a few more miles down the trail."

Billy planted the dirt-caked shovel and leaned on the sweaty handle as he rolled a smoke. He said, "Think we need to catch up with the Crooke boys, as quick as we can. We've pretty much taken our time up till now—what with gettin' out here and all. Better start humpin' it, if'n we want to keep them two crazy bastards from leaving any more dead folks sittin' around like storefront dummies, waiting for someone like us to find."

Carlton pulled his knife and started hacking at a nice piece of pine. "My glorious God, Billy, even if we go at it hammer and tong, that don't mean we can stop these murderous sons of bitches before they pull another killin' just like this one or worse."

"What do you want to do, Hayden?" Limber Hand stared into my eyes and waited for a decision from the person he had obviously decided was the leader of our group of dedicated man hunters.

Studied on our newest set of problems for about another minute. In a deadly silence that fell over us like a shroud, made up my mind to plunge ahead, but knew I had to be careful about what got said.

"Dennis, take up the trail again. Run it as far as you can. We'll hang back for another hour or so, catch you as soon as we finish here. If you get too far ahead, pull up, have a smoke and rest for an hour or so. We'll be coming on shortly."

He nodded, swung into the saddle, and kicked out of the gully and onto the open grasslands above us. I waited till the sound of his mount died away before turning to my friends. "Have something important I want to talk with you boys about." Led them away from Barking Dog's tent and stopped under a stunted oak.

Carlton looked puzzled when he said, "What's up, Hayden? I can always tell when you've got something on your mind. That jagged piece of flesh across your nose ole Saginaw Bob left on you has a tendency to get flushed when your blood's up."

"You boys take a seat here in the shade. This could well turn out to be the most important discussion we've had since I came on with Judge Parker. Roll yourself a smoke, get comfortable."

Once they'd wallowed themselves out a good spot to sit and put flame to tobacco, I started. "Gonna tell you boys something no one else knows, not even Elizabeth."

Carlton blew a cloud of cigar smoke my direction, left the stogie in the corner of his mouth, and went back to his whittling. "Hell, Tilden, this really does sound serious."

"Serious as it's likely to get, Carl. We're talking life or death, and how we go about it. Once I'm finished, the three of us are going to come to a joint agreement about the way we're doing our jobs."

Billy got impatient. "Well, get on with it. This tree

root's fine for a few minutes, but, if we're gonna be here very long, I'm gonna pull the saddle blanket off my horse and pad my skinny rump up some."

Pinned them both to their seats with as solemn a law-dog gaze as I could muster. "Other than Daniel Old Bear, I trust you two men more than any I know. And if Harry Tate still counted himself among the living, he'd be sitting here with you. Wanted you to know that up front. In spite of those feelings, and before we start in earnest, you've both got to swear that anything I tell you won't go any further than right here, right now. You've got to agree to that single condition, before we can talk about anything else."

They grinned, grumbled, and grumped around about how I could possibly question their loyalty and such, and finally held up their hands and swore before God they'd keep our discussion to themselves.

With that part out of the way, I jumped in on them with both feet. "For the past several years, rumors have floated around inside Parker's cadre of lawmen that Marshal Hayden Tilden was working out here on his own, with nothing to restrain him. You've both heard those stories."

A quick, knowing glance snapped between them. Billy arched an eyebrow. Carlton barely shook his head. The spare movement sent an easily interrupted message, and neither of them spoke.

"Well, I'm here to tell you the accounts you've heard are not *quite* correct. Everything I've done has been with the blessings of the judge and others in the court. Right after we got back from our shoot-out with the Dudley bunch down in Texas, Judge Parker called me to his office and gave me the responsibility, and awesome power, to go after the worst of the worst. He told me to bring them back, dead or alive. He also made it as clear as a dipper of rainwater that, as far as he was concerned, dead was just fine and dandy." Stopped and let what I'd said kind of seep into the cracks and settle around in their brains.

A big grin spread across Billy's face as he pointed at me. His cigarette dangled between yellow-stained fingers. "I knew it. Knew from the time we went out to Kingfisher Creek and kilt all them ole boys that was runnin' with Comanche Jack Duer. You tried to make it seem like I made the decision to rub them out. You're slipperier than a handful of tadpoles, Tilden."

Carlton jumped in with, "So, what the hell does it mean to us? We ain't got nobody's blessings to go around bustin' a cap on anyone we don't want to bring back. Hell, we don't get paid for the dead ones. Leave them out here under the grass, or let the wolves carry them off, and it's no money in our pocket. Most of us ain't independently wealthy like you, Hayden."

"I understand, Carlton. And I've got an offer for you. If you agree to what I'm about to propose, on any man-hunting trip we go on together, I'll pay you out of my own pocket, the same as if you'd done the work for the court. Same rate per mile traveled, same stipends for capture and return of prisoners, meals, transportation, and expenses—all of it. And you get to keep any rewards posted on those wanted dead or alive. All you have to do is agree with me that some of these men are so far beyond the realm of lawful reasonability that they should never be given the opportunity, or privilege, of appearing in Judge Parker's court. We can take care of any problem that arises out here exactly the way Billy described the other night. We'll find those responsible, push them into a fight, and kill them."

Carlton ran a nervous hand from his forehead to his chin. "That'd be taking the law into our own hands. We'd be actin' as judge, jury, and executioner. Sounds a lot like vigilante justice, carried to its badge-wearin' extreme, to me."

Billy's eyes darted from Carl's face to mine and back again. A mischievous grin flitted across his lips. "Hell, I ain't got no problem with that."

Carl scratched at his chin like a man in deep thought when I said, "Every time we have to pull a pistol, there's the chance we'll have to shoot somebody, or they'll get lucky and kill the hell out of us. The men who indulge in the kind of murder we've seen over the past few days don't deserve to be breathing the same air as decent people. And if we take the worst of these belly-dragging snakes back, there's always the chance some smooth-talking charlatan will keep Maledon from getting his hands on them."

Billy shook his finger at Carl and interrupted with, "Damn right. Men like the Crooke brothers don't need to be walking in the company of the living."

Could tell we still hadn't completely convinced Carlton yet, so I pressed on. "Personally, I think such men have a rendezvous with God, and all we'll be doing is helping them along to that glorious appointment with their individual destinies. Besides, Carl, have you ever brought in a murderer who didn't fight?"

He kicked at a tree root with the toe of his boot. "Don't think so. Cain't recollect one who just threw his hands in the air and come peaceable-like. Guess most of them boys figure they're gonna hang anyway, so why not go down, snapping and screaming, with all guns blazing. It's always a big deal for a murderin' outlaw son of a bitch to kill a couple of lawmen on the way to

Satan's doorstep. Beats having your neck stretched, while hundreds of half-drunk, hymn-singing gawkers watch you piss your pants. Cain't really say I blame them all that much."

"Ever been hurt by any of the men who resisted?"

"Oh, hell yes. Got scars all over my body from being beaten, shot, or stabbed by killers from Arkansas, Texas, Louisiana, *and* the Nations." He pulled the bandanna back from his neck and pointed, "Cotton McCay, from over near Shreveport, put this one on me with one of those .41-caliber pissant belly guns he had hid in his boot. Drilled his sorry ass four times. Still didn't kill him. But took my time bringing the wife-murderin' scum back, and he just naturally bled to death along the way. Course it might have had some effect on his health that he *accidentally* fell off his horse, and landed on his head, every so often, too."

Billy leaned against the tree trunk and laughed out loud. "Damn, Carl, that's exactly what Hayden's talking about. We go along with this, and you won't have to help one of them fall of his horse. We'll kill them outright and get it over with."

"Goddammit, I know what he's talking about, Billy. And, sure, we've all done something like what I've described, but, unless I'm mistaken, there's a bit of an added piece to what Hayden has in mind. I ain't never went out expecting to kill anyone deliberate-like. Always left the decision to die with them I was a-chasing. If the scurvy dogs want to resist, then I don't have any problem taking whatever action necessary to bring the festivities to an outcome designed to make certain I don't die in the process. But we're talking deliberate murder here."

Billy spit at a spider crawling up the tree root near

his hand. "Personally, never had much trouble killing a murderer. Most times, I felt mighty good afterward. Especially if the family of the person the son of a bitch put in the ground came up and told me how much they appreciated me bringing their misfortune and feelings of loss to a soul-satisfying conclusion. 'Bout the same as watchin' the life-stealin' sons of bitches hang as far as I'm concerned."

Knew I had Billy on board, so I locked eyes with Carlton and tried not to let him catch his breath. "If you don't want to go along with me on this, Carl, I totally understand. But we've chased bad men all over the Nations together, and this is the first time I can remember you developing something like a conscience over how murdering bastards meet their just deserts. Seems to me, you blasted the hell out of more than your share up in Red Rock Canyon two years ago. And just yesterday, you swore bloody vengeance on the Crooke boys yourself."

He picked pieces of tobacco from the chewed end of his cigar and flicked them onto the ground. "Damn right, and would do it again. Don't misunderstand me on this, boys. Ain't trying to weasel out on you here. Actually I pretty much agree with everything that's been said, so far. It's just, you've gotta admit, this is taking a conscious step over the edge, that most of us might have considered but kept to ourselves. We're talking about *deliberately* killing men we don't even know."

Billy cut loose with a dry, mocking laugh. "You know the sons of bitches, Carl. They're men like Saginaw Bob, Dangerous Dave Crowder, Morgan Bryce, Vander Lamorette, and a dozen others you've helped bring down. Sorry, thievin', child-murderin', lowlife, scum-sucking bastards to a man. There ain't a damned one of them worth the sweat off my horse Sneezer's big sorrel rump."

Figured we'd wrestled it around long enough, and the time had come for a decision. No point dragging it out any further. Pulled the six-inch bowie from my boot and said, "If you're with me on this, I propose we take a blood oath on it—right here, right now."

Both men glanced at each other, then back to me. Billy stood and held out his hand. Carlton stepped between us and did the same. I said, "You're sure about this, Carl? No doubts left? Nothing else troubling you?"

"Never had any doubts, Hayden. Just wanted to make certain we all understood exactly which way the wind was blowing, once we'd committed to the thing."

Billy gave him a friendly poke on the shoulder. "I knew you wouldn't snake out on us, Carl."

Used my knife for a razor, in a pinch, and didn't have any problem putting a nice scratch in each of our palms. Clasped Carlton's, then Billy's hand and made a short speech about us being brothers in blood, and that's how it started.

First thing Carlton said was, "Well, the deed's done. Now, let's find the Crooke boys. Put an end to 'em 'fore they rub out more innocent folks who just happen to cross their blood-soaked paths."

8

"They Took Turns Doin' the Nasty with Her"

WE PUT THE torch to Cyrus Barking Dog's booze hall on Crooked Man's Creek. Turned the tent, and everything in it, into a pile of impossible-to-identify ashes in less than an hour.

Billy cut the dead men's horses loose. He said, "They'll probably follow and graze along behind us. Got nowhere else to go. Be looking for a handful of grain come nightfall."

Carlton patted a tall bay mare on the nose, cut her loose, and slapped her rump. The animals all headed straight for the creek, fast as they could hoof it, when given the opportunity. Billy figured right. The thirsty beasts took some water and, like hungry orphans, trailed behind us when we pulled out.

Caught up with Limber Hand about three hours later.

He'd stopped and had his blanket flung out on a nice, soft mossy spot at the base of an elegant-looking elm tree. He stood and waved as we pulled up around him. Soon as our boots touched the ground, he hit us with the first good news we'd heard since we stepped off the train in Antlers.

"They've slowed down, Marshal Tilden. The new captive they took back at Barking Dog's is like an anchor dragging behind them. Either a woman or child, haven't been able to determine exactly which, yet. Doesn't matter. They keep going the way this trail reads, and we should have them in sight by late tomorrow afternoon. Some pretty rough going ahead. They're running from one gorge to the next. Think they've about worn their mounts down to the nub. Have to stop soon. That's when we'll make up a lot of ground."

Slow going for us, too. Got to a point where we had to dismount and lead the horses for five miles or so. Just before sundown, we pulled out of the trees, bunched along the edge of a deep cut. Ran on two men afoot, who stumbled right into the middle of us. Poor boys had been beaten to a pulp and were nekkid as the day their mamas brought them into the world.

Took about an hour for us to get them warmed up, settled down, and clothed with what extras in the way of shirts and pants we carried in our war bags. Since none of us had ever run across bloodied-up, totally nekkid fellers before, we couldn't wait to hear their story. Even though it slowed our progress considerably, we talked it over and decided to take the time and hear them out.

Carlton pulled out his tattered notepad and a stubby piece of pencil. He said, "Want you men to tell us what

happened. As much, or as little, as you can—right now.
Let's start with your names."

Ruddy-faced, stringy kid, who looked to be in his late
teens, held a hot coffee cup in both hands and said,
"Horace Porter, that's me." He jerked a thumb toward
his companion. "His name's Greely Holland. Greely
ain't very bright. Story went around back home as how
his mama dropped him on his head when he 'uz just a
young 'un. His pap used to beat the hell out of him ever
chance he got. Old man said he did it on account of
Greely being so stupid. Greely ain't stupid. Just not
overly bright. I brought him along with me to get him
away from the brute. He don't talk much. Just laughs
when he's happy, and grunts a lot, mainly. Guess it'd
be best if'n I tole the whole story. Ain't that right,
Greely?"

Holland's heavy eyelids went up and down like they
had anvils tied to them. He threw a slack-jawed glance
at his talkative friend. A tongue the size of a train con-
ductor's wallet lolled out one side of his mouth like a
sick dog's, licked across cracked lips, and dipped back
into the coffee cup.

"See," Porter said, "he's 'bout half as smart as a stack
of busted wagon spokes."

Carl looked up at me and shook his head. "Where
you boys from?"

"Me and Greely growed up in Hondo, Mississippi,
just a bit south of Memphis, Tennessee. Ever since we
wuz kids, we done heard as how you could get to a place
called Red Rock Canyon, out here in the Nations, and
maybe hook up with folks on they way out to Califoreny.
Figured we'd get ourselves over there. Pick up a burlap
tater bag of that gold we done heard 'bout what lays
around on the ground just a waitin' to be found."

Billy held his cup in one hand and tapped the lip with

an edgy finger. "You fellers are almost forty years late for that one. Gold rush days are long gone. Besides, our friend, Marshal Tilden, and some of us ole boys blowed the hell out of Red Rock Canyon a couple of years ago."

Porter glanced from one of our faces to the other. For about a second, his lopsided grin resembled that of his goofy friend. "Aw, you boys is just a-joshin'. My paw done tole me all about it ever since I wuz a nubbin. Said them streets in the City of Angels is paved a foot deep with the glitterin' stuff. So much gold dust in the dirt, hogs have snouts that sparkle and shine. You don't have to be a-pullin' my leg, and tryin' to keep me'n Greely from a-gettin' our share."

Carlton shook his head again and sounded exasperated when he asked, "How'd you and your friend get out here, Horace?"

"Walked, mostly." He put a hand over his mouth and whispered, "Had us a horse when we started out, but it up and died 'bout a week ago. Greely gets right upset if'n you talk about it. Probably a good thing you boys come along when you did. We 'uns wuz a-gettin' pert hongery, what with not havin' anything much to eat for two or three days now."

Carlton scratched his ear with the runty pencil and glanced at each of us as though seeking approval for anything he might be about to ask. "That's real interesting there, Horace. But what happened to you? Why are you boys all scratched up, bruised, beaten, and nekkid on top of all that?"

Our disheveled son of Mississippi sucked the crumbs from one of our leftover biscuits off his mud encrusted fingers, and smacked his lips like he had a chunk of my wife's angle food cake. His friend looked up and goofily smiled at the slurping sound.

"Yestiddy mornin' couple of fellers come up on our camp. We wuz mighty glad to see 'em. Being hongery and all, you know. 'Specially Greely. He don't do well 'thout somethin' in his big ole belt-strainin' belly. Wouldn't know it by lookin', but he can be pretty hard to get along with, if'n he ain't fed regular. Kinda like a wild dog, really. Well, we figured them fellers was a-gonna save us from starvin' to death."

Limber Hand jumped in with, "What did the men look like?"

"Oh, you know, just average. One wuz a bunch better dressed than t'other'ern. Fancy dresser seemed to be the leader. Second feller wasn't a bunch smarter'n Greely. Fact is, got to thinkin' for a spell there, as how he and Greely coulda been brothers. But, and this is some odd, I come to believe them two ole boys was actually related somehow. They never allowed as how. Course the liquor might've had something to do with the way they acted. That could well have made me guess wrong in some of the specifical particulars about 'em."

Billy said, "Drank a lot, did they?"

Porter glanced up at the stringy marshal with a fleeting sneer on his lips. Kind of look a man gets when he realizes he knows things you want to hear, and how much power you've given him by becoming his audience.

"Ain't never seen men suck down that much tornader juice afore in my entire life. I thought Greely's pap could drink, but them ole boys put him in the shade. They walked up to our campfire carryin' a bottle in each hand. Their mounts, and the ones them women was a ridin', was weighted down with the stuff. Wonder to me the poor horses could walk with the load they wuz a carryin'."

Limber Hand jumped forward and got right in the stunned boy's face. "You saw the women?"

Porter leaned as far away from the Choctaw policeman as he could get and muttered, "Yeah, I seen 'em. Couldn't miss 'em. Come in right behind the men. Young one rode up like she was the queen of Sheba, or somethin', what with that Injun lookin' blanket she had draped over her shoulders."

Limber Hand didn't let up. "Describe her for me—the young one."

"Looked to be Injun, far as I could tell. Just like you, maybe. Right pretty little thing. Long black hair tied in pigtails, either side of her head, with bloodred ribbons. Maybe thirteen, fourteen years old."

His head snapped around my direction when I asked, "Did she appear in good health, uninjured?"

"Seemed so, but the other poor gal wuz a mite older and in a bit worse shape. Looked like someone had beat the hell out of her. Whole bunch of 'em hadn't been in camp long, when them ole boys snatched the women off their horses. Took turns a-goin' at the older one right in front of anyone what wanted to watch."

Carl closed his eyes and asked the most obvious question. The one none of us really wanted to hear Porter answer. "Whaddaya mean by 'goin' at' the woman?"

The agitated boy looked embarrassed. "Well, you know. They took turns doin' the nasty with her, right there on the ground—and be goddamned boys, they made us watch."

Billy looked puzzled for a second. "I hear you right? You said they did the nasty with her, Horace?"

Porter sounded a bit testy when he snapped, "Yes, goddammit. Done the nasty on her. Took turns. First the big stupid 'un, then that other 'ern. Drinkin' an' a hollerin' like animals the whole time."

"Where was the Indian girl during the assault?" Dennis's voice dropped like a man beaten into the ground by the sudden realization of an ugly truth he'd rather not have to deal with.

Porter looked confused. "Assault? Warn't no assault. Didn't beat her up or nothin' like that. Hell, they wuz doin' nasty on her. Course they wuz some considerable rasselin' around, grabbin' and such at the same time. Tore her pantalets off and tied 'em 'round her neck. Jumped on her like a couple of hunchin' dogs."

Limber Hand's anger flared up. "Get to the question. Where was the pretty Indian girl during all the 'doin' nasty'?"

"Oh. She grabbed her blanket off'n one of the horses, fell down on the ground, and covered herself completely up with it. Could hear her moanin' like a baby at first. Then she started singin' one of them Injun songs. Words didn't make no sense. If'n they wuz words. Hard to tell, since we ain't got no Injuns livin' 'round our part of the country."

I kneeled beside the shaking boy and tried not to get him any more excited than he already was. "Horace, how did you and your friend get all beat up the way you are? Something must have happened after all the rasselin' and such."

He glanced into my eyes, then at each of his past questioners. Boy might have been dumb enough to think he could drive nails in a snow bank, but he could tell when his captive audience was genuinely interested in what he had to say. A look of beaming pride swept over his face.

"Well, they finally settled down some, after a-jumpin'

that gal, 'cause they made her put food on the fire. Indian gal didn't cook, but them boys forced her to
serve'm like she was a slave or somethin'. Me'n Greely
wuz damned glad to see all that food goin' 'round, you
know. But the bastards didn't let us have much of what
got cooked up. Just the leftover scraps and such. Afterward, both of 'em got to hittin' them jugs again and,
quicker'n a pickpocket at a prayer meetin', they wuz
drunker'n Cooter Brown and madder'n hell on a tree
sledge. Don't think liquor treated 'em fellers well a-tall.
More they drank, the crazier they got. That big dumb
one couldn't keep his pecker in his pants for more'n a
minute, or so. Seemed like he spent most of his time on
top of that older lady during the whole dance."

Our agitated witness stopped a second and gestured
at the pile of cold biscuits again, as if to ask for another.
Carlton handed him two. The boy took one for himself.
Gave the second to his gawking friend. Fine gesture
when you think about it much. Both smiled and looked
like they'd just cut into a piece of medium-rare beefsteak
the size of a wagon wheel.

"We watched 'em run around camp like dogs, howl
at the moon, jump on that older lady another time or
two, and just generally act like they'd gone moonstruck
crazier'n a mason jar full of lightnin' bugs. Scared the
hell out of me. Greely might be teched, but he wuz
scared, too. Cried during most of the humpin' cause he
couldn't understand it, you know." He motioned toward
Limber Hand with his coffee cup. "Girl with the braids
covered herself up with that blanket again and wouldn't
come out. Thought them two loons wuz finished, when
they got done jumpin' that poor gal, but the one in the
fancy shirt said for us to take our clothes off. Started

screamin' like a gut-shot panther and told us to get nekkid, nekkid, nekkid."

His memory of the event caused his hand to shake more as he bit off another piece of the biscuit and fished it from one side of his mouth to the other. "Guess we didn't do it fast enough for 'im. Crazy son of a bitch snatched up a big ole switch and went to whippin' our asses like we wuz his redheaded stepchildren or somethin'. When we wuz finally nekkid as plucked jaybirds, and already had bloody marks from that tree limb all over us, he give us each a knife. Tole us to start a-fightin'."

I'd seen men amazed by the brutality they had to witness, endure, and investigate. But, as God is my witness, don't think shocked astonishment ever sat on the faces of anyone like it did on Carlton, Billy, and Dennis Limber Hand that night. Our flickering fire sent stabbing waves of light from one man's dumbfounded gaze to the next. Guess the crazed image of those poor Mississippi clod kickers, buck-assed nekkid, slicing at each other with knives, while being whipped with switches, was more than they could get their minds wrapped around. Given the events of our previous couple of days, don't think anything would have surprised me. Especially after the nightmare I'd had about Bob Magruder.

"Course, Greely didn't understand what the hell he wuz supposed to be doing at first. Mighty embarrassed. Probably the first time, since he wuz a baby, anyone had seen him 'thout his clothes a-coverin' him up." He put a crumb-covered hand over a biscuit-stuffed mouth, leaned away from his friend, and whispered, "Big son of a bitch has one of them tiny little thangs, you know. Might have about as many brains as a tin cup full of creek water, but I think he's always been some embarrassed by it."

Carlton moaned. Billy got up and walked off into the dark. "Gonna check on the horses," he said and waved at us over his shoulder as he headed into the trees where we'd staked our animals.

Horace looked hurt. His pained expression exposed a man who reveled in the audience he'd built, and how much he hated to lose even one. Must've figured he'd better get to the point, or we'd all get tired of his tale and wander off in search of Billy.

I tried to put him back on track with, "Did they threaten to kill you, at any point, during all this madness?"

"Oh, hell yes, 'bout every other breath, one or the other of 'em said he'd shoot hell out of us, or chop off our heads with an ax, or cut our cods off, set us on fire, or somethin' just as bad."

Carl turned his head away from the conversation. Heard him murmur, "Sweet Jesus. There anything as bad as havin' your cods cut off?"

"Well, me'n Greely flopped around, made a few passes at each other like we wuz serious about the thang, and eventually, them evil bastards got so drunk they passed out. So, we 'uns shucked them knives and headed for the bushes. Didn't even stop to pick up our clothes. Heard that little Injun gal squealin', 'take me with you, take me with you.' But we couldn't."

Horace's head dropped till his chin rested on a heaving chest. He got shifty eyed. I could tell the beaten farm boy was thoroughly embarrassed by his inability to help a woman he knew was in the most desperate kind of distress.

Finally, he glanced up at me with tears in his eyes.

"You understand don't you, Mr. Marshal? Took ever-thang we could do just to save ourselves from them crazy bastards."

Limber Hand perked up again. "You could've cut Myron and Byron's throats while they slept."

Porter rested his head in his hands like a man shamed by the verbal face slapping. "Thought of that 'un, too. Never kilt nobody afore, boys. Damned bloody business cuttin' a man's throat. Nasty way to do a killin' on a feller. If'n we'd had us a gun, think I coulda shot me at least one of 'em, but bet the other'n woulda woke up, kilt me and Greely quicker'n double greased lightning. So, we headed for the trees. Run till we couldn't run no more. Got up and run again. It were mighty hard on nekkid fellers runnin' 'round in the dark, like that. Damned sticker bushes cut us up worse than the switchin'. We heard 'em stumblin' round in the brush tryin' to find us. Sons of bitches wuz too drunk. And them woods wuz dark'n the inside of a dead cow. Did as much fallin' down and cussin' as anything. We'd been wanderin' around all night like lost sheep, when you fellers found us. Y'all hadn't come along, guess we'd of just died out here somewheres. Coyotes would've had our bones for supper. Turnin' up as coyote dung's a damned poor way to go out, far as I'm concerned."

Think all us lawmen decided, at almost the same instant, we'd heard all we needed. Carlton pulled me out to the picket line. Billy sidled up and listened as Carlton said, "What're we gonna do with them, Hayden? If we take 'em with us, they're gonna slow us down a bunch."

Billy said, "I'll catch each of them one of the horses we turned loose back at Barking Dog's. Being as how they got all the way out here on the back of a single animal, it should help them along on their trip considerably."

Thought it over for a bit before I added, "Believe we should give them the horses, whatever food we can spare, some pocket money, and head them back to Fort Smith. You're absolutely right, Carl, we can't take them with us, and if they head west, they'll end up deader than hoe handles."

So that's the way the plan shook out. Billy roped a ride for each man. He said, "Hayden, neither one of these poor boys would know horse shit from wild honey. If they make it back to town alive, it'll be nothing short of a God-sent miracle." Secretly, I pretty much agreed with him, but couldn't see any other way out of the thing.

Carlton cooked those boys a sack of biscuits and added enough dried beef to do till they could make it to any town along the way. We pointed them toward Arkansas. Told them to keep the sun on their faces every morning, and things would eventually work out fine. I gave Horace a note and directions to Reed's Store. Told him to ask for Elizabeth. Figured she could find some work for the misguided wretches and, maybe, we could eventually get them back to Mississippi. Still feel today exactly the way I did then. People that dumb don't ever need to travel too far from home.

Carlton had each man make his mark at the end of the deposition he wrote in his book. We waved them out of camp and prayed the luckless plowboys made it back to civilization alive.

Next day, about an hour past noontime, the trail led us to a rambling, newly built cabin sitting within spitting distance of the Washita. Structure looked five, maybe six rooms at most. Even from a quarter mile away, the lumber was so green you could almost smell it. We hid ourselves in a stand of oak and walnut trees and watched the place through our long glasses for almost an hour, while Limber Hand scouted his way around to the far side.

His efforts didn't help us much. When he got back, only thing he could say was, "Lots of tracks in every direction. Might be as many as half a dozen men down there. Counted eight saddle horses in a corral out back. Looks to me like they've been moving animals, of every kind, in and out of here on a pretty regular basis. Probably stealing ponies from everyone within fifty miles. Been rumors for months that a new bunch of bandits was operating from these parts. Guess we might have accidentally found the thieving scum."

Carlton puffed at his handmade. "You think our bunch is inside with this horse-stealin' crew?"

"Far as I can determine, right now. I'd have to scout out a good ways further west than I had time for to be absolutely certain on that one."

Course Billy itched for a fight and let his feelings be known without being asked. "Think we should march right down there. Call them boys out." He half-cocked a pistol and spun the cylinder on the sleeve of his shirt.

Carlton grinned. "I'm with Marshal Billy Bird. Let's arrest them as wants to go back alive. Kill those what don't." He said it, twirled a pistol on his finger, and dropped it back into a well-oiled holster strapped high on his right hip.

Dennis looked like he'd been slapped. "What if Precious is down there? We go charging in like a herd of range-crazed steers in a liquor store full of glass bottles, they could decide to murder her, outright."

Tried not to alarm him too much when I said, "You

know as well as we do, anything could happen anytime, Dennis. Right now, we're fairly certain the Crooke brothers' trail leads to the cabin. Little doubt about it." Everyone nodded their agreement. "Only way we'll ever find out for sure if she's inside is go down and have a look. Got to let God take a hand in these proceedings every so often. Now seems like one of those times."

Carlton picked at his fingernails with a pocketknife and said, "Hayden, why don't you and me go over there and talk with anyone willing. Limber Hand and Billy can hang back, stay hid, and keep us covered. That way, whoever's over there won't know for sure how many of us there really is."

I glanced from Billy to Limber Hand and said, "What do you boys think about Carl's plan?"

Billy didn't even bat an eye. "Sounds good. But I swear if there's even the hint of gunfire, I'll open up with everything I'm carrying." He slapped the butts of both those Schofield pistols with the heels of his hands.

Limber Hand nodded his agreement. I pulled the .45-70 from its bindings. Always felt better with the big beast in hand, rather than a pistol, anytime the unknowns and unknowables outweighed what I could put a definite finger on.

But Carlton said, "Better give that buffalo-killing cannon to Limber Hand, Hayden. Be easier for him to cover us from here. Take your scattergun. You know how much bad boys hate those things."

Handed the rifle to Dennis and grabbed the two-barreled blaster. For my birthday that year Elizabeth had presented me with a beautiful gold inlayed and engraved model 1878 Colt ten-gauge shotgun, with exposed double hammers and twenty-eight-inch barrels. That morning was the first time I'd had occasion to pull it. Truth be known, I hated to use such a magnificent weapon for the dirty business we did out in the Nations.

Carlton and I strolled to within fifty feet of the rickety shack's poorly constructed door. Drew to a stop beside a nice-sized oak near the riverbank—just in case we needed some quick cover.

A pair of poorly attended horses was tied to a hitch rail out front. Bay mare switched her tail at tormenting flies biting on her powerfully built rump. Muscles rippled under her glossy hide and sent the insects buzzing off, only to quickly return and start the whole process all over again. Her neighbor, a buckskin gelding every bit of sixteen hands, stamped a back foot and, every so often, tossed his head around. Mounds of dung gave the appearance the animals had been standing in place for some time.

Entire area was mighty quiet. No dogs, cats, chickens, or other animals in evidence. Couldn't see the penned horses Dennis mentioned. Smoke coming pretty steady from a galvanized pipe poked through the roof. You could hear the river rippling over rocks and snags—way too quiet for my taste.

Carl shouted, "Hello, the house. You have deputy U.S. marshals out here on official business. We'd like to talk. Send someone out."

We could hear a heated discussion inside the shack that lasted almost a minute. Occupants must have been trying to keep their voices low, but didn't have much luck with it. Know I heard a "goddamn" at least three times. Rough door opened to a foot-wide crack and a thundering voice roared, "How the hell do we know you be what you say you be?"

Carlton snapped back, "We're Deputy U.S. Marshals Carlton J. Cecil and Hayden Tilden from Judge Parker's court in Fort Smith. Someone in that rat's nest has surely heard of us. We have John Doe warrants in hand and can serve on every damned one of you light-fearing sons of bitches. So stop wasting our time and get a spokesman out here so we can chew the fat."

Good bit more frenzied yammering went on behind those sap-leaking green planks before the rugged entrance gradually creaked open and two men stepped outside. I couldn't believe what happened next.

Carlton sucked in a sharp breath, took a step backward, almost tripped, and whispered, "Sweet jumpin' Jesus."

Startled me to the point where I reached out and put my hand on his arm. "What is it, Carl? What's the matter?"

His eyes blinked real fast and darted from man to man as if he couldn't believe what he saw. "Hayden, that big son of a bitch is Cassius Striker, and the other one's his baby brother Farkas. If the devil and his favorite imp have faces, we're looking right at the evil sons of bitches. You and I've run across some rough cobs over the years, but nothing as bad these boys. We've just stepped into buffalo patties up to our knees. Let's get out of here, and damned quick."

9

"Just Who in the Hell Did They Eat?"

FOR THE BEST part of a minute the whole world got so quiet I could hear my own hair growing. Studied the rough-looking men as thoroughly as I could from where we stood, cut a glance at my partner, and said, "Hell, Carl, I've never heard of Cassius Striker, or his baby brother. Don't think anyone would ever forget a name like Farkas once they heard it. Know for damned sure I won't."

Carlton held his pistols behind him and cocked both weapons at the same time. He tapped the barrels against the backs of his legs, talked fast and low, and never took his eyes off the surly-looking pair. "They're from an earlier era—back before you showed up in Fort Smith. Disappeared four, maybe five years ago. Rumor I heard, at the time, claimed they got into an argument with a bunch of down-on-their-luck types over in Texas near Adobe Walls. Everyone thought they'd been killed deader'n rotten fence posts and had new jobs shoveling coal in the furnaces of hell. Tale that made most folk the happiest said them Texicans had chopped off ole Cassius's head and stuck it on a pole. Least that's what we all hoped had happened. Goes to prove the old adage, you should never believe anything you hear and only half of what you can see with your very own eyes."

The largest of the leather-clad couple had barely been able to squeeze his enormous bulk through the poorly constructed door frame. A flowing black beard, streaked with long white waves, cascaded down his chest, and stopped about an inch above the polished silver buckle on a double-rowed cartridge belt. Pistol butts jutted from the folds of his ragged, fringe sleeved coat in the old Hickok, no holsters, gunfighter manner. A wide-brimmed, filth-covered felt hat nestled so far down on his brow I couldn't see his eyes, but I knew we were being measured from head to foot for a hole in the ground next to the corral in back.

The hairy varmint to the monster's right, and slightly behind him, looked almost the same, even down to his choice of pistol rigs. Only ascertainable difference was one of proportion. From what I could see, you'd have needed twins of baby brother Farkas to make one mammoth Cassius.

The big man bellowed, "Well, here we be. You badge-totin' skunks called this here prayer meetin'. Git to jawin'. What you John Laws want? You done interrupted our afternoon repast, and we'd like to git back to it. Rabbit stew ain't a-gittin' any warmer while you're wastin' our time out here shootin' the shit with you bastards."

The open belligerence caused Cecil to get more nervous by the second, and he didn't seem inclined to say
much once he realized which big, vicious cat we had
accidentally grabbed by the tail. So I jumped in with,
"We're looking for a pair of murderers named Crooke
from over near Phantom Hill. If they're inside, we want
them—and right by God now."

Smaller of those piles of greasy leather yelped, "What
in the blue-eyed hell makes you thank they's around
here 'bouts?" Even his voice was a study in brotherly
contrasts. The monstrous Cassius Striker sounded like a
man talking from the bottom of a quarter-filled metal
rain barrel. His unfortunate little brother had a voice you
could, in the dark, easily have mistaken for that of a ten-
year-old girl's, high-pitched, squeaky, and downright
silly sounding. Caused a serious grin to creak across my
ironbound, lawdog countenance.

Cecil shot a quick glance my way and must have read
my mind. He whispered, "Stories I've heard claim he's
killed a dozen men over remarks, real or imagined, about
his girly-soundin' speech patterns, Hayden. I'd be careful about smilin' much, and for the love of God, please
don't laugh. We'll be pitchin' lead sure as hell's hot and
icicles are cold."

Figured we didn't have any choice but to keep moving forward. No point in backing up from where we
were. Yelled, "We followed the Crooke brothers from
Phantom Hill in the Choctaw Nation to your front door,
boys. Over the past week those men have murdered at
least seven people. We intend to take them to Fort Smith
for trial at Judge Parker's convenience, and a hanging
at George Maledon's pleasure. But if they insist, we'll
kill them right here. Just a matter of which one you, and
they, choose."

Course I lied about escorting those fellers back to civilization. They were dead men, as far as the Brotherhood and I were concerned. All it would take to accomplish such a desirable end was an open shot or two. Decided if the Striker brothers wanted to get crossways of our efforts, we'd oblige. They just might have to be rubbed out along with the Crookes and we'd be happy to send them to Satan. But I figured it wasn't the right time to tell them how I really felt about their tenuous place in God's great plan for the future.

The mountainous Cassius leaned backward to hear more whisperings from his miniature brother. He hooked his thumbs behind the fully loaded cartridge belt and bellowed, "Them boys wuz here last night. We fed 'em and waved good-bye early this morning." He gestured absently toward the river. "If'n you want 'em as bad as you say, best strike out west along the Washita. Should be able to catch 'em by dark or breakfast tomorrow. Think I mighta heard one of 'em say something about stopping over at Willow Bend for a spell. Good water, nice and cool there. They's even a small shack to put up in fer the night. It's on your way to Boilin' Springs. Shouldn't take you more'n three or four hours to catch up with 'em."

That's when Carl surprised the hell out of me and dropped the big one on them. "What about the women?" Shocked me right down to the rowels on my spurs. Honest to God, didn't think he would do it. Not after all his heated warnings about those bad boys.

You could see the surprise on the Strikers' bearded faces, even as far away as our position. More heated whispering went on for almost a minute. Boys spent way too much time on the answer we finally got.

"Don't know nothing 'bout no women. Didn't see no

women. Them fellers was alone when they stopped, and we fed 'em. You lawdogs will have to take up any missing Indian females with the Crooke brothers, when you catch up with 'em."

I whispered, "You believe that, Carl?"

"Not one damnable mendacious word. He's lying like a buffalo rug in the lobby of a Denver whorehouse. Besides, don't think I said anything about *missing* Indian women. Just women."

Tried my best to make it sound like we'd got all the information we wanted and had decided to set out west as quick as fast horses could carry us. "We thank you for your cooperation, sir. Hope we didn't keep you from your rabbit stew too long. Please be on the lookout for one or two women alone. Appreciate if you guided them to us for their safety."

They grunted like irritated hogs and jerked the door back on its squealing leather hinges. Farkas Striker stepped inside ahead of his mammoth brother. For a moment, so brief I wasn't sure it actually occurred, a face emerged from, and then receded back into, the depths of the shack's inner darkness. An otherworldly visage, like an oil painting on a museum wall, framed by black braids tied with bloodred ribbons.

"Carl, did you see what I just saw?"

"Yeah. That looked an awful lot like Precious Tall Dog to me. If not, she must have a twin sister living with the Striker brothers. Now that would be one hell of a far-fetched accident of fate and coincidence, wouldn't it?"

Weapons at the ready, we backed our way into the tree line. Makeshift burlap curtains, on both of the shack's saddlebag-sized front windows, moved from side to side as the occupants kept an eye on our departure. Soon as we managed to get out of sight, and back into some degree of safety, Carlton staggered to a dead stump and flopped down like a man exhausted.

Placed my free hand on his shoulder and said, "We're fine for now, Carl."

Limber Hand abandoned his hiding place and came running over. He sucked in several deep breaths and said, "Well, what do you think, marshals?"

Cecil holstered shaking pistols and wiped his brow with a bandanna. He said, "Think we've got one hell of a problem on our hands, Dennis. That's Cassius Striker and brother Farkas over there."

Billy walked up, and soon as he heard the name Cassius Striker, the boy snapped to attention like a member of the 7th Cavalry waiting to get past Saint Peter at the Pearly Gates. "You sure about that, Carl?" His voice contained the same awe, and fear, I'd heard in Cecil's when he first laid eyes on the filth-encrusted, oily brothers.

I finally popped a garter or something. "What in the hell is it about these men that sets you boys' teeth on edge so?"

Carlton looked at me like he'd just heard the most pitifully ignorant wretch in the world say something a thousand miles beyond stupidity. He lifted his hat and ran shaking fingers through his hair. "Before they kind of vanished from the scene, rumor that followed them bad boys, all over the Nations, was that they weren't above eating anyone they killed." He eyed me nervously for a second, then stared at the ground. "Hell, Hayden, I don't worry much about ending up dead while doing this work. Ain't no point in letting your mind dwell on the thing. That kind of worrying could drive a man to distraction. But being eaten afterward, by the likes of the Striker brothers, does give a man reason to pause and reflect."

Limber Hand sighed. "Ah, so they're the ones. Heard about those men years ago. When we were kids, my friend's parents used to scare them with the Striker brothers. Said if the children didn't behave, the Strikers would come in the night, sneak into the teepee, carry them away, cook them in an iron pot, and pick their teeth with the bones." His voice gradually descended into what sounded like a man telling the most horrible ghost story he'd ever heard.

"Sounds like a cartload of steaming fresh horse manure to me," I snorted.

Billy pulled at my sleeve and as serious as a man holding a sack of diamondback rattlesnakes said, "No, Hayden, everyone who's been out here, for any time at all, has heard about the Strikers and is scared shitless of them."

Couldn't believe my ears or eyes. Men I respected; men who'd fought blazing pistol battles by my side; men who stood up with me at my wedding; now they acted like ten-year-old kids scared by their parents' favorite boogeyman. There we stood, meaner than seven kinds of hell, armed to the teeth, kicking around something as idiotic as whether the Striker brothers were cannibals or not.

Carlton and Billy looked at me like I'd slapped them when I said, "Well, just who in the hell did they eat? Can you boys name at least one of the folks the Strikers cooked up and wolfed down? Do we have tintypes or miniature oil portraits of anybody who ended up in their stew pot? Do they like turnips with old Aunt Nellie?"

"Dammit, Hayden," Carlton grumped, "this pair of evil animals are dangerous sons of bitches. Been known to eat the folks they kill. This ain't even close to amusing. These scum-sucking dogs are well known for such barbaric behavior. Damn near every individual in the Nations has a favorite horror story they like to tell about these men. If the Strikers kill you, they'll eat you. Damned unnerving thing to think about."

"Didn't say anything I've heard today was funny, amusing, entertaining, droll, or comical, Carl," I shot back. "And you still haven't answered my question."

Billy took a peacemaking tone and said, "Way I heard it, them Striker boys got caught in the worst blizzard in a hundred years up in the Rockies. Happened one winter back in the early '70s, while on their way to California. Party was starving, so the Strikers killed everyone. Ate all of 'em just to stay alive. Cooked those poor folks in a big iron pot with some taters and just the right seasoning. Stew, and what they hung up in a makeshift smokehouse, kept them murderin' savages alive for more than a month." He shook his head and mumbled off with, "Makes a body shudder just to think about going into a strange smokehouse, don't it?"

Carlton shook his head and sounded disgusted. "No, hell no, Billy, that ain't the way it happened. I got the real and actual true story from somebody who was in the company. Seen the whole thing. A trusted man of my acquaintance claimed to have been there at the time, told me the Strikers and a party of their fellow buffalo hunters got hemmed in by some Apaches at a desert watering hole in northern New Mexico. Injuns kept them pinned down so long the Striker boys killed at least one of their friends and ate him while the others watched in disgusted shock and horror. That's the bona fide and *only* factual story of how them boys earned a reputation as man-eaters. And I'm here to tell you, Carlton J. Cecil don't want nothing to do with them today, tomorrow, or next week, by God."

Rubbed my aching temples and said, "Look, boys, I don't care if they've barbecued half the population of Arkansas out on Judge Parker's courthouse lawn and served them up with beans and corn on the cob. They're just men, and if what Carlton and I saw, when the door opened, was real, we might have to kill both of them, and anyone else that's inside that shack helping them. Besides, this whole bag of frog feathers sounds suspiciously like the kind of thing some of these lawless sons of bitches are good at. They inflate their reputations with bullshit just to make people more afraid of them. You know I'm right. Hell, John Wesley Hardin claimed to have killed fifty-two people down in Texas, before the Rangers jerked him up short. Most bodies anyone could legitimately account for on his part, was eleven or twelve. Personally, I don't give any credence to Hardin's crock of bull whizzers, or what I've heard so far of the Striker brother's wad of blanket fuzz."

Limber Hand listened to our hen fight like a paralyzed man standing in an open field, enthralled by the approach of a coming cyclone that would, in all probability, deposit his dead body in another territory, or state, hundreds of miles away. When I finally got around to the part about having seen his daughter's ghostly face in the open doorway, he went buggier than a mattress full of brown dog ticks. Distraught lawman made a sound like a wounded buffalo and started on a run for the rugged shack. Only managed about three steps before Billy tackled him. We had to hold Precious Tall Dog's father down to keep him from charging out into the open and very surely getting himself, and some of us, shot to pieces.

Billy and Carlton each latched on to an arm. I grabbed him by the chin and said, "Trust me on this, Dennis. The three of us fully understand how you feel about the girl. But we can't go running out of these trees, burn up boot leather over to their door, and start demanding they give her up. She'd be dead, for damned sure, before we got halfway to the river."

Took a minute or so of struggling, but he knew I was right. My stern reminder calmed him considerably. Once I felt fairly certain he and my friends had their emotions under control, the basics for a plan of action started to take shape.

After considerable cussin' and discussin', we settled on a plot Billy was first to put forward. Each of us nodded his agreement. I mapped the raid out so everyone would be totally informed and understood his individual part in the coming action.

Scratched out our plan in the sandy soil with a broken twig and said, "So here's what we're gonna do, boys. Dennis will take the horses, lead them west along the Washita, for at least five miles, before he crosses to the north side and doubles back around the cabin to low water, about a mile east of our present position. Once there, he'll wade over to this side again, hoof it back for a rendezvous as quick as he can. He'll hide the horses among these trees and join up with me, since I'll be closest to the house. While he's doing that, the two of you pick a good spot, watch and wait for the right opportunity to present itself. We're gonna hope someone inside hears our horses move off, assume we've left for Willow Bend, and come out to make sure. That'll split them up, give us better odds in any fracas that might develop."

Let that all sit on them for a few seconds before I

continued with, "If we hear a woman scream at any point, everyone moves in at the same time. If that happens, be careful, but get as close as you can, and blast the hell out of anything moving that don't look female and isn't me."

Thought we'd decided on the whole shebang, before I went to the trouble of laying it all out. But just about the time my traveling doo-dah show and shooting match was set in motion, Limber Hand grew a stubborn streak. Decided he should stay and one of us should make the diversionary run. Can't say anyone faulted his judgment, or feelings, on the matter. If my wife or daughter got caught in the same position, be damned if I'd have left the scene no matter what anyone else said, including Hayden Tilden.

Guess Billy and Carlton reasoned all this out about the same way. Neither put up much of an argument. And Billy quickly volunteered to make the run with the horses. Since Dennis seemed to have calmed down, after his initial outburst, I allowed it. But, secretly, figured I'd better keep a weather eye on the man. If he let his emotions lay too much of a hold on him, his actions might get Precious, and the rest of us, killed.

When Billy got everything headed up and moved out, Dennis, Carlton, and I parted company so we could set up in carefully selected watch spots at various points around the shack. Once we were in place, no one could have entered, or left, without drawing our attention.

My *compadres* agreed to wait for my signal before attempting any kind of rescue. Course the whole plan depended on the hope that moving our horses would draw some of the inhabitants out to investigate. That way we'd have fewer to deal with in a fight. Figured if we could get whoever was inside moving around, it'd give us a better idea of how many there actually were and what kind of opposition we could expect.

But it seems like some things just never work out the way you think they will. No matter how well you plan a gunfight, it can go to hell on you in a damned big hurry. Always pays to be careful—real careful.

Found a nice mossy spot behind an outcropping of rock about a hundred yards from the cabin's front entrance. Made it possible for me to comfortably lie down, have a clear and unobstructed view of the shack, and get a stable rest for the rifle. A covering of huckleberry bushes and stunted trees made it virtually impossible for anyone inside the shack to spot me. I missed Caesar. He'd hightailed it right after we found those poor dead folks in the trees. Probably back in Fort Smith by the time we came on the Strikers.

Dennis and Carlton did a good job moving into their chosen hidey-holes. Only caught brief glimpses of them as they flanked the object of our attention in search of a good spot. Don't think I'd have noticed either man if I hadn't really been looking for him.

Barely got the Winchester and my shotgun laid out for quick use when the door popped open and Farkas Striker poked his ugly head into the afternoon sunlight like a loggerhead turtle on a shady riverbank. He stood kind of halfway in, halfway out, warily stared into the dusty sunshine, then pulled back into the darkness.

After nearly a minute of studying all the bushes, trees, and most of the rocks within sight, he turned and spoke to someone inside. While I couldn't hear exactly what was said, the sound of his voice indicated some irritation, and the longer he talked, the louder and more contentious the discussion got. Eventually he nodded, pitched what looked like a tin cup back inside, slammed the plank door, and stomped over to the bay mare tied at the hitch rail.

Cloud of dung flies whose meal had been interrupted fogged up around Farkas. He jerked his hat off and swatted at them like a man who'd been attacked by angry bees. I was able to make out most what he said that time—bluest kind of language. During the entire outburst, I had his head behind the front sight of the .45–70. Could've easily splattered his pea-sized brains all over the ground. Dung flies would've had a field day.

Striker's filth-encrusted behind had barely hit the saddle when the door burst open again and big brother Cassius stumbled out. Swung the Winchester around his direction; soon had him lined up and ready to be measured for a hole in the ground. Then the bearded brigand did something completely unexpected. He jerked a piece of rope from a peg on the wall and tied the door shut—from the outside. Jumped on the buckskin and kicked it west along the river. Sure as shooting, our plan had worked. They were on the scout to see where we'd gone.

About a minute after they headed for points west, a thought hit me. There couldn't be any more of their type inside. Who in his right mind would want to ride with men known as cannibals? No one. Cassius Striker had tied the door in an attempt to keep somebody from getting out, and that somebody had to be Precious Tall Dog.

Pulled my big-ticking, two-dollar Ingersoll pocket watch out of my vest and let ten minutes pass before I decided to take advantage of the situation. Didn't hear a sound or detect any movement during the entire time. Discarded the Winchester for the shotgun. Pulled the hammers back on both barrels, and stepped away from the rocks. Did the closest thing to an imitation of Billy

Bird you can imagine. Strode directly to the door of the shack, as fast as I could walk, and didn't slow down till I'd kicked it off its leather hinges. Stood on the flimsy threshold just long enough for my eyes to adjust to the light. Boldly stepped inside behind the open muzzle of Elizabeth's spanking-new gold-plated present.

A rude table made from the same planks used to build the rickety structure and several rawhide chairs sat in the middle of a dirt-floored room. The rough-cut walls still smelled of pine, and glistening, golden brown sap ran from many of them. Some enterprising soul had used the tacky wood juice to post torn pages from the corset ads of a Montgomery Ward mail-order catalogue all over the place. Obscene comments and crude drawings had been added to the faded pages with a pencil. A potbellied stove in the far corner contained a rapidly dying fire. Food-encrusted tin plates and dirty cups lay scattered on the table and every other flat surface available. A broken-down Hoosier balanced on unsteady legs near the stove, and a variety of field creatures scurried about the garbage-covered floor. Dust fogged in around me and swirled on the shack's fetid air, in the manner of storm clouds passing over the flatlands of Kansas. Like a panther hit with a branding iron, I jumped at the first door on my left that led out of the trash-littered room.

Precious Tall Dog lay on an iron bed pushed to the back wall of the windowless space. Her hands and feet were tied to each of the brass topped corner posts. The Striker brothers had her naked body stretched out so tight her back barely touched the mattress. Lengths of coarse new rope cut into her flesh, and small drops of crusted blood pooled on the surface of the corn-shuck mattress beneath her ankles and wrists. The greasy gag in her mouth had drawn more blood from bruised and cracked lips.

Her eyes darted from the top of my head, to the shotgun in my hands, and looked as big as dinner plates. She panicked, squealed into the gag, and twisted in an effort to get away from me. Considering what my mind's eye conjured up by way of the manner she'd probably been treated by other men, I couldn't blame the frightened girl in the least.

Leaned over and whispered, "Precious, Precious, I'm a friend of Dennis Limber Hand. He's waiting, outside. I'll take you to him." Stream of soft-spoken words seemed to calm her.

Worked as fast as I was able. Given she couldn't help much, it took a bit more effort on my part to get her loose. Knew Limber Hand would be right behind me—and pretty damned quick if I didn't get out soon. Didn't want him to see his daughter strung up like that. No father should ever have to see such a thing.

Snatched the razor-sharp bowie out of my boot top, sliced her free quicker than a Civil War surgeon with a bone saw, and wrapped her in a blanket so fast she barely had time to realize what was going on. Jerked her into my arms like she didn't weigh any more than a six-year-old child, and headed for the safety of the trees.

10

"LET'S SADDLE THIS BROOMTAIL AND SEE WHICH WAY SHE JUMPS"

THE WHOLE SPONTANEOUS raid couldn't have taken more than two minutes. Didn't stop running till I delivered Precious Tall Dog back to the safety of my original hiding place. Dennis arrived less than ten seconds later and had the girl cradled in his arms. He whispered in her ear, sang to her like she'd not yet reached her first birthday, and tears streamed down his face.

For the very first time, God brought it home to me in no uncertain terms that Indian folk just might care as much for their children as I did for mine. The shaken man's love for his daughter hit me hard, and reminded me I had a wife and son I loved, who patiently awaited my return back where at least some civilization resided, and men like the Striker brothers were nothing more than lurid stories in Fort Smith newspapers or shoddy dime novels.

While my impulsive behavior had solved one precarious predicament, it created a far more dangerous one. Carlton recognized the dilemma immediately. He pulled me aside, watched Dennis and Precious over my shoulder, and under his breath said, "Hayden, we've got to get away from here. Them Striker boys won't follow Billy's bluff far before they come running back. They ain't gonna leave a pretty little plaything like her for long, and God help us when them flesh-eatin' sons of Satan discover we've done took her back. No two ways about it, there's gonna be hell to pay."

"Damn, Carl, just didn't think past saving her, once I realized she was in there alone. But you are dead-on right. We've got to scorch some trees in Billy's direction. Try to catch him when he crosses back over the Washita, and hope the Strikers don't find us before we can rendezvous."

Went back to the shack and rummaged around till I found the girl's discarded clothing. Her father got her dressed, then we hoofed it for the low water. Carlton and I brought up the rear, while Dennis tried to keep Precious moving, but she was in pretty sorry shape and couldn't set the kind of pace we needed. Limber Hand finally took her up piggyback, which helped considerably. When he tired, I carried her for a spell, then Carl, and so on till we finally reached the spot on the river where we'd planned for Billy to make good his return.

Found a likely spot to fort up behind a pile of rocks, just a few hundred feet from the riverbank. Some small trees here and there helped. Had a good view of the entire area where any attack would likely originate. Didn't have to wait long. Seemed as if we'd only been there a few minutes. Everyone still breathed hard when a voice from the trees boomed out like a field mortar.

"You badge-totin' bastards done took somethin' don't belong to you." Cassius Striker's words rumbled across a hundred-yard stretch of open ground like a rolling blast of Kansas thunder. Sound sent chills up and down my sweat-soaked spine. "She wuz bought and paid fer. Fifty dollars in solid gold coin. She's our twitch, and by God we'll have her back. Even if that means killin' every damned one of you thievin', badge-wearin' sons of bitches."

A hundred yards south of Cassius, I heard Farkas's squeaky voice as he barked, "Goddamned right. Y'all done went and took the wrong woman. She's mine and brother Cassius's, damn yer eyes, and we'll take her back, even if we have to kill all of you."

Carlton shook like a man in the grips of the ague, but he yelled back, "Don't know whether you ignorant jackasses know it or not, but you can't buy and sell people anymore. That's what the big war was all about. Remember that one, you dumb bastards?"

A hysterical quality had crept into Farkas Striker's voice next time he spoke. "Goddamn you, she's mine, and if'n you don't give her back we'll murder the hell out of all you do-rights in the most horrible way you can imagine. Then I'll cook your livers and gizzards with some wild onions and prairie sage. It'll make damned fine eatin'."

Guess Cassius figured his little brother had gone too far. He snapped, "Shut the hell up with that silly-assed stuff, Farkas. These men are gonna be real reasonable-like and turn the girl over to us 'uns. They knows how horrible it'll be if'n they doesn't."

Limber Hand's voice sounded like it floated acros

that field on a river of ice. "Either one of you feel like you're man enough, come on over, take her back. Otherwise, get on your horses and get away from this place as fast as you can ride."

Cackling laughter from the trees caused the return of that prickling sensation up and down my back. The hair stood on my arms, and Carlton moaned like someone had just pulled a couple of his teeth with red-hot horseshoe tongs.

Shifted the Winchester onto my lap and pulled a panatela from my vest pocket. Between puffs to light it, I said, "Reckon it'd do any good to meet Cassius out in the field and talk with him?"

Carlton grabbed my smoke and took several puffs before handing it back. "Gonna make out like I didn't hear what you just said, Hayden. Them ole boys are nuttier'n one of my grandma Mathilda Cecil's Christmas fruitcakes. Step from behind these rocks, and we'll be digging a grave for you when this is all over."

"No, I'm serious, Carl. What if I can get Cassius to come out of hiding and meet me to talk all this over. Soon as he's in range, I'll drill the hell out of him a time or two. That just might bring Farkas out of hiding, and you can blast him to kingdom come when he shows."

Carlton flashed a foxy grin. Got shifty eyed and said, "That's mighty damned devious, Tilden. Sounds exactly like the kind of stuff Cassius would pull, given the chance. Actually, think I love hell out of it. If he agrees to show himself, you can just about bet he plans on killing you as soon as you're close enough. That is, if he doesn't gun you about a second after show your face."

"He won't do that, Carl. Don't judge he'll do anything but talk with me. Or, at least, think he's going to talk."

"Why not?"

"Well, when we step out, he's got to believe that if he shoots me you boys won't ever give Precious up. Should keep him in line till I can put him down, don't you think?"

He and Limber Hand went into their chin-scratching routines and spent way too long thinking the plan over. Finally, Dennis said, "I believe it'll work, Carl. Besides, you can keep your gun on Cassius, just in case he gets a belly full of bedsprings. Give me the .45-70, Hayden. I'll take care of Farkas when he shows himself."

Carl looked at me like a man staring right into the eyes of death. "You're sure about this? Don't want to think it over a bit longer?" He leaned closer and got extra whispery serious when he said, "You know that if he kills you, he'll eat you, Tilden."

"Aw hell, Carl, that's the most ridiculous thing I've ever heard. And, no, I don't want to think about it any more than I already have. Let's saddle this broomtail and see which way she jumps. You boys get sighted in. Don't want any missed shots here when the blasting starts. Quick as I get in range, I'll plug Cassius. If I miss, Carl, you shear his pin, and don't waste any time doing it. When Farkas shows his ugly face, Dennis, you bust his pack as soon as you've got a shot. This train is moving on down the track. Everyone on board?"

They both nodded, but Carl couldn't help arguing his point right up to the end. "Might be ridiculous, but Farkas has already said he'd fry up your liver." He grabbed my hand, squeezed, and whispered at me again. "Be careful, my friend. Wouldn't want to be the one who has to tell Elizabeth you done gone and got et up by the Striker brothers."

Cupped my hand over my mouth and yelled, "Mr. Striker, will you come out and talk this over with me?"

Ole Cassius didn't waste on his reply. "Ain't nothin' to talk over, lawdog. You're holdin' our property, and we want it back." About what I expected, but his voice contained the hint of a man who just might be willing to come my direction.

Winked at Carl and Dennis, pulled a lungful of smoke from my cigar, and blew it into the air. "That's what I want to talk about. I'll leave my guns here, and we'll try to come to an agreement."

From our left Farkas chipped in with, "Don't be a-listenin' to him, Cassius. He's that scar-faced son of a bitch we seen back at the cabin. I don't trust him any further'n I can throw a frozen horse. Man has the look of death on him."

Figured I'd let them think on my proposition for a spell. A minute or two of silence passed. "Well, what about it, Mr. Striker? Can we talk, or are you gonna listen to your whining little brother?"

Must have hit home with that one. Farkas was beside himself when he yelped, "You can go to hell. You and all the rest of Parker's bunch of law-bringin' killers," he screeched.

Cassius put an end to the argument with, "Shut the hell up, Farkas. I'm trying to think over here." After a few more minutes, an almost reasonable-sounding elder Striker yelled, "Come on out, Marshal. I'll meet you halfway."

"You first, Mr. Striker."

Only thing I could figure was that ole Cassius had developed a lust for Precious Tall Dog's young flesh so powerful, and wanted her back so bad, gambling with his life seemed reasonable. Otherwise, I don't believe he would have ever abandoned the comfort of a mighty fine hiding place. He shuffled from behind the safety of the tree line. Carried a rifle across his arm, completely exposed himself, and even took several tentative steps our direction before he stopped.

"Your turn, lawdog. Ain't coming any farther till you show yourself." He'd stopped not more than a good jump or two from a sizable rock. Looked to be leaning that way, when I stood and moved toward him. Held my hands up, palms out. Had left all my weapons in a heap at my feet. All but one of Handsome Harry's ivory-handled Colts. Shoved it under my cartridge belt in the small of my back.

Tried to make him comfortable by all my observable actions. Even went about twice as far his direction as he'd come in mine. But, as distant as we were from each other, I could detect a look of pleasure spreading across his fiendish face. The uncomfortable feel of a poor decision began to scratch some purchase in my agitated brain. Remember thinking to myself, well, Tilden, you've finally done it this time. Done gone and made the beautiful Elizabeth a widow and young Tommy an orphan.

Took two or three minutes for us to get to a point where I figured he was in death-dealing pistol range. But I never had a coon dog's chance in hell of pulling down on him. A rifle shot from behind me burned past my ear like a nest of angry yellow-jacket wasps and punched a black hole the size of my thumb between his eyes. A gushing stream of hot black blood spurted out a foot from his head like beer from a freshly tapped saloon spigot. Man dropped to his knees. Still had the rifle clutched to his chest in an ironclad grip. An odd, un-settling grin tickled the edges of his lips, and one of his eyes closed as though winking at me.

Heard him scream, and turned just in time to see a crazed Farkas jump from the cover of trees off to my left. He yelled, "You murderin' sons of bitches," and fired three rapidly levered shots my direction. First two went wild, but the third kicked up dust at my feet, knocked a heel off my boot, and let me know he had the range. Jerked my pistol, dropped to the ground, and pressed myself out as flat as a week-old cow flop. Knew I didn't have a chance in hell of hitting him from that distance, but wanted to let him know I'd be trying.

Demented dirtbag started running toward me. "How is it with you, Cassius? Have they kilt you, brother?" I rose just enough to bring the gun around, but before I could fire, Carlton and Limber Hand dropped a black curtain of lead that knocked ole Farkas sidewise and put him on one knee. But hell, that didn't come close to stopping him. He cut loose with a couple of extremely well-placed blasts designed to keep anxious friends low, jumped up, and heeled for me again. Guess he'd man-aged to stumble about ten more steps when the next barrage from the rocks spun him around like a kid's top. Shooting and spinning at the same time, he finally dropped to both knees. His chest heaved and sucked with the numerous holes Cecil and Dennis put in him. Couldn't believe my eyes, but he used the rifle as a crutch, pushed himself erect, and tried to stand again.

Guess Carlton had seen all he needed to see and knew all he needed to know of the Striker brothers. Might have been the innate fear he had of being eaten by them, or maybe just the blood lust of the moment. Can't really say which. All I know for sure is, he jumped from behind our rocky stronghold in a dead run and didn't stop till he was less than ten feet from the still struggling Farkas.

Pointed his rifle at the wounded man and said, "Why ain't you dead yet, you murderin', rapin', people-eatin' son of a bitch?"

Limber Hand strolled up beside Carlton like a Baptist preacher about to give a Sunday sermon. Gently pushed him aside with the barrel of my Winchester rifle, took careful aim, and before I could get there to stop him, sent Farkas Striker to St. Peter and his Golden Book for judgment. Tore his ticket for an express iron horse ride to the Great Beyond with a well-placed slug to the left side of his head that bore out the right, brought a good portion of his gnat-sized brain with it, and splattered the whole shebang all over hell and gone.

Carlton clapped Dennis on the back and said, "Damned fine shot. Got him just about the exact spot I had in mind." He took a couple of steps toward the still quivering body, bent over and said, "You still in there, Farkas? St. Peter put you on the road to perdition yet? Can you see the gates of hell by any chance? If you can, would you mind describing them for me, so I can share your personal experience with others of your ilk? Should make a grand lesson for those who don't want to walk the straight and narrow. Come on, now, Farkas. Know you can do it."

I had to stop him, or he'd probably have gone on for an hour or so. Carl never was one to whoa up on his own once he got on one of his tirades. "That's enough, Carl. He's not even quivering anymore. Can't hear a word you're saying. Nothing left here but the husk."

He eased the hammer down on his Winchester. "Damned good thing. Thought there for a minute Dennis hadn't managed to finish him off. Don't generally shoot a man once he's down, but with this son of a bitch I was more than willing to make an exception."

While Carl and I made preparations to bury the Strikers, Limber Hand tended his trembling, speechless daughter. He whispered to her in what I took to be their language. Couldn't understand, myself, but it sounded an awful lot like he just wanted her to know she didn't have to think about the men who'd abused her—ever again.

Once I'd had a moment or two to think on it, his efforts reminded me of the time I rescued Missy Talbot from Schmoker Pratt and Comanche Jack Duer, and how that effort sealed something deeper and far more than run of the mill friendship. Said a little prayer under my breath that the girl would recover as well as Missy.

Billy led the animals back across the Washita about two hours after our dance with the Strikers ended. He slid off his horse and shook his head in disappointment. "Damn, Carl, I know this was your doing. Couldn't you have waited till I made it back?" He lit a hand-rolled. "I mean, hell, it would've been kinda nice if you could've just held off for an hour or two. Now I ain't gonna be able to brag about killing the best-known man-eaters in the Nations. Yep, from now on Carlton J. Cecil is gonna have to live with the reputation of being the sanctified eradicator of infamous cannibals. Bet by this time next week, the *Elevator* will be referring to you as Carlton J. Cecil, famed slayer of people eaters." That's when I had to step in and put an end to it.

"Boys, no one can ever know what went on here today. This falls under the heading of efforts by the Brotherhood of Blood and can't be talked about once we leave here. Not even in whispers. Don't matter if people know we killed them, but no one can ever even suspect we executed the sorry bastards. Understand?"

Could tell by their quizzical looks that appreciating the politics of the situation didn't rate real high on their list of priorities at that exact moment. Carl turned his palms up and shrugged. Billy shook his head and stared at the ground, then looked up and said, "You're right, Hayden. If people find out we just up and decided to kill these sons of bitches, we'll have to explain everything that led up to it. We could end up in court arguing with lawyers for years to come. Course you realize, this means we're gonna for damned sure have to find the Crooke brothers and make certain they're good and dead, too."

He'd barely made the observation when Limber Hand sidled up, took me by the arm, and led me away to a more private spot. His hands shook as he removed his hat and stood holding it in front of him.

"Marshal Tilden, my daughter is in a bad way. While I'd give almost anything to be there when you find the Crooke boys, I need to get her back to civilization. Chickasha's a few miles closer to our present position, but I know for sure there's a fine doctor over in Tecumseh. If you have no objections, I'm gonna head that way soon as I can get her on one the extra horses."

Pain in the man's voice was heartbreaking to hear. Placed my hand on his shoulder and said, "Dennis, I can't think of a single reason for you to spend another minute on this evil chase. But you've got to promise me no one will ever know, exactly, what went on here today. You can tell anyone who asks that we tracked the Crooke brothers to the Strikers' cabin, rescued Precious, and had to kill the Striker boys in the process. Far as we're concerned, both these boys died in a toe-to-toe pistol fight that they lost. Understand?"

"Yes. Completely. Don't worry, sir, I owe you more than I can ever repay. It'll be exactly as you wish."

"And don't trouble your mind over the Crooke brothers. We'll find them, no matter how far they run. And when we do, no one will ever see them again. They'll pay dearly for what they put your daughter through. Hope we can find them soon enough to save the other woman, too."

He shook my hand, Indian fashion, nodded, and less than an hour later was nothing more than memories and a wispy cloud of reddish-orange dust. Billy, Carlton, and I had taken Cassius Striker's advice. Headed north along the Washita for Willow Bend—beautiful, almost Eden-like spot, in those days. How could we have imagined the dreadful reality waiting for us there? The kind of death and horror every lawman in the West always dreaded most.

11

"THOUGHT I WUZ IN HEAVEN THERE FER A MINUTE"

WE PUSHED HARD till it got too dark to go on. Camped about ten miles south of Willow Bend, and made the last rump-buster of a run early the next day. By the time we arrived, the sun had got up pretty good and blazed like Satan's fireplace. Weather had been right forgiving up till then. But it got hotter than the hinges on hell's front gate that morning. Horses lathered up, and all of us sweated our boots full. Billy commented as how he believed the Striker boys had arrived in perdition, and when them people-eatin' sinners shook hands with Beelzebub it caused the flames in the pit to flare in celebration.

From a hill overlooking one of the Washita's numerous natural oxbows, we laid on our stomachs and, carefully, eyeballed the entire area, before making any impetuous moves. Our fellow marshals from the Parker court, and anyone else just passing, frequently used the abandoned cabin located there for temporary refuge. Rough shelter hardly rated being called a cabin, though. More like a finished-out lean-to in the advanced stages of weather-induced dilapidation. Stock pen of split rails and uprooted bushes barely kept the animals hemmed in at night.

Billy squinted into his pair of much-used cavalry binoculars and said, "Glad they didn't make it to Boiling Springs. Wasn't looking forward to that dance. Does that look like a man sitting under the sycamore tree by the corral to either of you boys?"

"Been watching him ever since our feet hit the ground," Carlton said, as he adjusted the length of his long glass. "It's a man for damned sure, but if he's moved any, I haven't been able to detect it. Something familiar about him, but I can't quite put my finger on it yet." He turned his telescope, glanced at the larger end of the glass, and said, "Good God, there's a gob of grease on here that would make it impossible to recognize Buffalo Bill if he was right in front of me." He pulled out his bandanna, spit on the lens, and started rubbing.

I'd been zeroed in on the area between the back of the slapdash shelter and the river. Tall patch of big bluestem grass grew in the apex of the crescent and had suffered from the movement of a good many animals. It appeared someone had crossed over to the north side pushing a herd.

Personally held serious doubts the murderous Crooke brothers remained anywhere within ten miles of us. I figured the wicked bastards had most likely headed out at sunrise. Hoped that was the case. Horses, or cows, or both, would certainly slow them down. In my estimation, taking on a trail herd seemed a poor move for men on the run.

But if I'd learned anything in my man-hunting experiences, it had to be that you could never predict what killers might do. Wouldn't have surprised me if both the murdering loons decided to wear anvils for hats and iron skillets for drawers.

Swung my glass to the tree Billy and Carlton had mentioned. Almost passed out when I realized they'd found someone we knew. "Jesus, that's Bixley Conner down there, boys." Popped out of me so fast it startled both of them.

Billy's cavalry surplus field binoculars couldn't bring the scene in as close as my spy piece. He snatched the eighteen-inch scope from my hands and extended it out to its full length. "Sweet merciful Father, Carlton. Hayden's right. It's ole Bix for certain. By God, if someone's murdered that man, I'll chase them to that horned boogeyman's front parlor and kill the bastards sure as big yeller dogs live in Arkansas."

Carl shifted around on his elbow and looked me directly in the eye. "Place looks abandoned, Hayden. If that's Bix down there, we'd better get moving."

None of us liked the situation we found ourselves in, but Carl's assessment was right as rain. Minutes could mean the difference between life and death, if our friend was badly wounded. We saddled up and rode in like a Comanche war party. Everyone bristled with cocked pistols, primed and ready for a blazing gunfight.

I made it to Bix first. Pulled Gunpowder to a jumping stop right beside him. Bounced off that big sorrel's back like a piece of coiled steel fresh from the fire. Dropped to one knee and untied his neckerchief. He moaned, swatted weakly at my hand with blood-encrusted fingers.

There was a considerable hole just above the lower pocket of his vest. His breeches were soaked with blood from the waist to his knee. Both his pistols lay in the dirt beside him. Billy tossed me a full canteen. I dabbed at our wounded friend's swollen lips with a soaked bandanna. Took almost five minutes, but he eventually came around to something approaching lucidity.

Few more minutes and ole Bix got to talking like a man who thought he could count on living for a hundred years. Through a bloody froth he muttered, "Damnation. Thought I wuz . . . in heaven there fer a . . . minute. You boys got a lot of goddamned nerve . . . a-draggin' me back from the other side . . . to this hellhole." He coughed, grimaced, and his bloody hand went to the hole in his side. "One of them . . . night-slinking sons of bitches shot me, Hayden. Don't guess I should . . . be surprised, what with all that lead flying around . . . in the dark. Think them egg-sucking dogs might have killed . . . all three of the other deputies."

Carlton ambled over from the cabin, holstered his pistols, and said, "He's right. There's three bodies inside— all wearing badges. Recognized two of them. Third feller must have been a last-minute posse man pulled in just for this trip. Can't say as I've ever seen him before."

Bix leaned on his free hand and tried to shift his weight to something more comfortable. "Ah, dammit all, that hurts. Hate gettin' shot."

"What the hell happened here, Bix?" Billy sounded like a man who chose not to believe his eyes or ears. Three dead deputies, and a wounded Bixley Conner, sorely tested the limits of his capacity for understanding. A man he respected and admired lay at his feet clutching a wound that could well prove fatal. Others he knew and liked lay dead as a pile of rusty horseshoes a short distance away.

Carlton pulled Bix's vest and shirt aside. I started on what little we could do to help him. Within ten minutes, we'd washed the wound and applied a bulky compression bandage over the hole. Slowed the leakage down a mite, but, my God, he'd already lost a tubful of blood. He kept talking the whole time. Surprisingly his voice got stronger. Sounded like a man afraid he might not get it all out.

"Me, Jack Tatum, Earl Gray, and that new one, Spuds Buckner, chased Charlie Two Knives . . . and his boys down . . . 'bout ten miles south of Minco Springs . . . other day. Were on our way back to Fort Smith. Stopped over for a night's rest . . . under a roof." He coughed and motioned for the canteen. I dribbled some water on his lips, but didn't want to let him hold it, for fear he'd suck down too much at one time.

You could hear the admiration in Billy Bird's voice when he said, "Damn, Bix, you caught Charlie Two Knives? Lawmen from all over Texas, Arkansas, and Louisiana have been after that odiferous skunk for years. Hell, he must be worth a couple of thousand dollars from the M.K. & T. Railroad, all by his lonesome."

"Yeah, we caught him, Billy. He and . . . that bunch of two-tailed . . . weasels of his got drunk, lazy, and stupid . . . all at the same time. Found the whole damnable bunch of 'em . . . passed out in a grassy gully, three or . . . four days ago. Walked up on 'em . . . and didn't even fire a shot. Thought it . . . was one of the cleanest catches . . . I'd ever made . . . in all my years a-marshalin' fer Judge Parker."

Carlton placed half of a lit cigarette between Bix's lips and wondered aloud, "But what happened here, partner? If you had them roped and tied, how'd they get loose?"

Bix moaned and grabbed at the hole in his side again. "We arrived . . . late yesterday afternoon," he gasped. "Always liked it here. Fine spot . . . to stop over, rest up from a hard run. After supper, I shackled . . . one of those bad boys . . . to each of us lawmen . . . for the night. Been doing the same thing . . . ever since we first caught 'em. Took Two Knives . . . myself. Figured he was the most dangerous . . . of the group and . . . would be less trouble, if he was my responsibility." He shook his head. "Didn't figure on them . . . other fellers showin' up."

Billy lifted the burning short from Bix's lips and replaced it with a fresh smoke. Carl mopped at the wounded man's brow with a damp piece of rag.

Billy said, "Who are you talking about, Bix? What other fellers?" We had a damned fine idea who'd attacked Bix and been responsible for killing the others. But the question gave our wounded friend something to think about, other than the fact that his life was surely leaking into the ground.

"Not for . . . certain sure, Billy. So damned dark . . . I couldn't see much of anything. Just know that during the night, men we . . . never would have expected . . . showed up . . . and all hell broke loose. They got to me first. Charlie and me was closest to the door. I woke up with . . . a gun barrel in my ear, and someone . . . riffling through my pockets for . . . the key to Charlie's shackles.

"Soon as ole Charlie got loose, he came up . . . with a pistol from somewheres. Started shooting . . . at anything moving. Screaming and dying like that's . . . an awful thing to hear. I rolled out to this tree . . . tried to plug 'em . . . on their way through the door. So much

. . . pistol work going on, I'm not sure who shot me."
He moaned again, a pained grimace washed over his
face.

"Christ Almighty, guess I . . . could have plugged
myself . . . in all the excitement. Now, wouldn't . . . that
be something? I can see the headlines . . . in the *Elevator*: Marshal Bixley Conner Shoots His Own Self—
Famed Killer Escapes." He waved his bloody hand as
though setting the type.

Carlton shook his head. "Nobody's gonna blame you
for this one, Bix. We followed the Crooke brothers to
that hill over yonder. They've been on a lethal rip that's
left a string of bodies all the way from Antlers to here.
Bet my horse, it was them boys what broke in on you
and got everyone killed. Poor dumb bastards probably
didn't have any idea how bad a bunch they was a-
turning loose when they did it. Crooke boys are newly
christened killers compared to Two Knives and his
bunch. Nothing but amateurs in spite of their abundant
recent murders."

Bix must have had all he could take. He passed out
colder than a frozen railroad spike. I put Carlton to
watching over our wounded friend. Sent Billy to scout
the tracks. From up on the hill, the trail looked like it
would be an easy one to follow. Examined each of the
men in the cabin myself.

Jack Tatum never even had a chance to draw his pistol. His clawlike hand was wrapped around its walnut
grips, tighter than the lid on a jar of store-bought pickles.
A bullet hole pierced his left eyebrow. Man looked
mighty surprised. Didn't relish telling his wife and six
kids about Jack's murder. Family had a rough time making ends meet, even when he managed a good trip to
the Nations. Couldn't begin to imagine what his death

would mean to Mrs. Tatum and all his barefooted kids.

Found Earl Gray lying on his stomach. Somebody had planted a butcher knife in his chest, all the way up to the wooden handles. He must've fought mighty hard. Several of the fingers on both hands were missing. Probably grabbed the blade of that fat-shanked meat carver during the fight. Cost me a minute or two, but I took the time and located all those severed digits. Stuck them in his bloody shirt pocket.

Spuds Buckner had crawled into a corner and been shot to pieces. Poor dead bastard held a pistol in each hand, but had only managed to get off five shots. I counted three holes in the man's chest and one in his cheek. Might've been others, but that was all I could see, at the time. They were more than enough to kill him. Damned shame for a man to die on his first trip into the Nations as a deputy marshal—crying damned shame.

Remembered seeing an announcement of Buckner's upcoming nuptials in the *Fort Smith Elevator,* two or three weeks before we went out looking for the Crooke boys. He had planned to marry the Reverend Hill's daughter, Janet. Used to see her in Elizabeth's store. A honey-blond, blue-eyed beauty that had the kind of smile could make grown men stutter and act foolish.

Carlton and I had started working on a travois for Bix when Billy fogged back in. He jumped from his horse before the animal stopped. "Gonna be easy to run this bunch to ground. With all of our dead friend's horses, the Crooke boys, and the other woman, they're moving pretty slow. Should be able to catch up with 'em in four or five hours, if we really push it."

Carlton slapped a dusty leg with his crushed hat and said, "Well, gonna be mighty damned hard to push much with Bix wounded like this. Can't leave him here. Need to get the man to Chickasha. He's lost so much blood I'm not sure he'll make it, no matter what we do."

We debated on our best course of action, for about ten minutes. Argued over who should take Bix back, and which of us should carry on our search for the killers. Billy held the straws. Carlton got the short one. Man was madder than a red-eyed cow.

"Goddammit, boys, every time we do this straw-drawing shit, I end up losing. Might as well go around with a short one in my vest pocket. Pull it out anytime there's a decision has to be made about who *won't* get to continue with the chase."

Billy smiled and egged him on. "Hell, Carl, I know a witchy woman over in Siloam Springs can sell you some good luck. Won't cost much. Hear you can buy a year's worth, for as little as ten dollars. Has to be in gold coin, though. She won't take paper money."

Didn't even slow Carlton down. He stomped to his horse, jerked the cinch strap on his saddle, and snapped, "While I'm at it, think I'm gonna go to the hospital in Fort Smith and take some nurse's training. Always having to drag one of you poor wounded sons of bitches back to civilization. Might as well get me some instruction on how best to treat you when you're down."

Billy and I exchanged winks. I piled on with, "Reckon you could wear one of those adorable little nurse caps and a white apron, Carl?"

He shot me a nasty look and said, "While I'm at it, think I'll get that carpenter over on Towson Avenue to build me a portable trail drag I can strap to the back of my horse. Carry the contraption around with me everywhere I go. Might as well be prepared to haul you wounded never-sweats all over hell and yonder in comfort."

Cussed a blue streak, griped, and kicked anything within leg range. Billy finally got tired of listening and said, "Why don't you give it a rest, Carl. Damnation, man, Hayden and I are gonna have to dig three more graves for them poor ole boys in the cabin. Personally, I'm getting damned tired of planting folks the Crooke boys have rubbed out. This keeps up, I plan to stop in the next town we pass and buy myself a new shovel."

Well, that one got us all to giggling like kids. And somewhere between the cussing and laughing, Bix Conner settled the whole dustup for us. Went to check on his dressings and, be damned, if he hadn't already quit this earth for a heavenly reward. Hit us all pretty hard. Hell, he didn't have one of those sucking chest wounds or a hole in the head. But the one scratch that pack of murdering scum put in him was just the right size to kill the man.

Judge Parker had introduced me to Bix my first day on the job, back in '79. Stout, bear of a marshal brought me out into the Nations and showed me the ropes. I genuinely liked the man. Everybody did. Ole Bix probably didn't have a real enemy in the whole world. Be willing to bet a sock full of money the man who killed him would say the same thing. As the years passed, the three of us did a lot of agonized second-guessing over his death. Always wondered if we could we have saved him. Damn, if we'd just gotten to Willow Bend an hour earlier.

When we threw the last shovel of dirt on Bix and his posse, Billy handed me my volume of Shakespeare and said, "You've gotta find something nice for Bix, Hayden. Man like him deserves a first-rate send-off—kind that takes him to God on the wings of beautiful words. All of these men deserve it. Can't think of any better way than to hear you read Mr. Shakespeare over their pitiful graves. Pick something fine for these poor dead boys."

Took me a couple of minutes or so, but I settled on a few carefully selected passages from *Richard II*—re-arranged to suit the time and place, of course. Glanced at my companions and said, "This one is going to be hard, my friends. Hope you approve of what I've chosen."

Then, in a voice rattled by emotion, I read, " ' . . . Nothing can we call our own but death, And that small model of the barren earth which serves as paste and cover to our bones. Let us sit upon the ground and tell sad stories of the death of kings: How some have been deposed, some slain in war, some haunted by the ghosts they have deposed, some poisoned by their wives, some sleeping killed. Oh, that I were as great as my grief, or lesser than my name, or that I could forget what I have been, or not remember what I must be now. Oh, call back yesterday, bid time return."

For about a minute after I finished, we stood silently in our dirty boots, and stared at grimy fingernails, and the freshly turned earth. Overwhelming feelings of loss were colored by the stark realization that this could have easily been any one of us, covered in dirt and waiting for the worms.

Billy surprised Carlton and me when he said, "Do you reckon it would be agreeable if I offered a prayer, Hayden?"

Carlton never looked up, but nodded his approval. "Think that would be right fine, Billy," I said.

He held his hat next to his heart and gazed skyward

as cotton-bowl clouds raced over us. "Our most gracious and forgivin' heavenly Father, we've seen the worst imaginable in men over the past week or so. Many good, God-fearin' people have died by their blood-drenched hands. These boys were our friends—their departure from this earthly life the result of foul and treacherous murder. Help us now in our grief. Harden our hearts for the task ahead, and give us the strength to carry on with the dangerous work we choose to follow. Please be good to ole Bix while he's with you. He was a fine feller, and we'll miss him. Amen."

Carlton stuffed his hat on his head and said, "Amen. Now let's chase these wild dogs down and put an end to this before any more innocent people have to die. Don't know 'bout you boys, but I'm damned tired of findin' the bodies left by these murderin' sons of bitches."

12

"YOU CAN SHOOT THROUGH ME WITH THAT BIG RIFLE"

WE HIT THE north side of the Washita, some east of Chickasha, in a dead run. Scorched miles of grass that came to our mount's bellies in an effort to make up as much ground as possible. The way Carlton had it figured, Two Knives and the Crooke boys had more than half a day's lead. Only good thing going our direction appeared to be those killers' lack of concern about leaving an easily followed trail. Sad truth of the matter held that if you were as evil as everyone knew those boys were, then you didn't have to worry all that much about who might be following you—a little maybe, but not much.

Guess we'd hoofed it around ten miles or so when Billy pulled up and asked for my long glass. After a few seconds searching the ground out ahead of us, he handed it back, pointed at a lone oak perched on a hill nearby, and said, "Look up there under that tree, Hayden. More bodies, I'd bet."

Checking that gruesome spot slowed us down a bunch. Band we were chasing had laid some boys out on the ground, as if they were on display at a funereal home in Fort Smith. Dead fellers looked all primed and ready to have commemorative pictures taken for family and friends. Their cold hands crossed over unmoving chests. Someone had even washed their faces and placed wildflowers between stiff, lifeless fingers. Remember thinking of it as the kind of thing a woman might do for the unfortunate departed left on the ground for possums and coyotes to feed on.

Carlton popped sweat-soaked reins against his palm. Then he pointed with them and said, "Bet you my next month's pay, and commissions, that one is none other than Ugly Bob Wildwood."

Since none of us knew the man by sight, the bet sounded like a safe one to me. Hell, he was a revolting-looking wretch. And the dirtiest human being I'd ever seen—living or dead. Had to hold my bandanna over my mouth and nose while we examined his filthy remains. Man smelled awful, and it wasn't just because he'd been dead for a spell. He just naturally stunk like a goat pasture in July.

Thing that convinced us we had certainly stumbled on the real, true, and only Ugly Bob was a letter Billy found in the smelly stiff's vest pocket. Surprised all of us the dead man even had the education or half the brain matter required to read and write. Maybe he couldn't do either, but the carefully lettered missive was addressed to Mr. Robert Wildwood, Esquire, and posted by a sister, Nellie Wildwood Dixon, who lived near Cherokee in the

Great Smoky Mountains of North Carolina. Not much in the note other than family business—hard life, quick death, and lack of money. Mrs. Dixon implored her brother to send anything he could, as their parents had hit upon something worse than bad times and couldn't hold out much longer.

"Don't guess she'll be hearing from Ugly Bob anytime soon," Carlton said as he folded the single sheet of rough paper and slipped it into his own inside vest pocket. "I'll pen a note to her when we get back to Fort Smith. She has a right to know what happened to her worthless brother. Won't mention how sorry he'd become, or how he died. Guess she deserves that much, even if he don't."

Billy said, "Long as we're betting, I'd be willing to throw down all the yellow money in my poke this other one is Erazmo Gadsen. Everybody always called him Raz. Know for a fact he traveled with Two Knives on occasion. Brought him in for horse theft about three years ago myself. But, good God Almighty, he's aged badly. That hole in the bottom of his face don't help his looks any either." Billy sneered and flipped a still burning cigarette stub at the dead man. "Big ole .45 took out part of his jaw and most of his teeth. Bet that one hurt like hell, didn't it, Raz?"

Carlton walked over and toed the second corpse. "How do you suppose they got plugged? You reckon maybe Bix managed to shoot both these ole boys before someone popped a cap on him back at Willow Bend?"

Considerable studying went on about that blessed possibility before I said, "Could be, Carlton. Or it could be they shot each other in the dark. Or, hell, maybe Two Knives decided he had way too many people trailing along behind him on their dash for freedom. To tell the

God's truth, don't matter much to me what happened to them. Just more problems we don't have to deal with."

Billy snorted, "Me neither. But, personally, I hope Bix was the one that killed both of 'em. And oh, by the way, fellers, I ain't burying these sons of bitches. They can lay right here and rot for all I care. Hope rabid wolves carry their stinking outlaw selves off, and scatter the bones all over hell and this half of the Nations."

Swung back into my saddle and said, "We don't have the time to bury them anyway, Billy. The Crookes and Two Knives still have a captive woman in their party. I truly fear if we don't catch them pretty damned quick, she'll be the next one we discover under a tree somewhere. That's one Shakespeare reading I'm not looking forward to. So, let's get moving, run this bunch of barn weasels to ground as quick as we can."

Trail turned back east not long after we discovered Wildwood and Gadsen. Went about ten miles and swung south. Carlton hovered over the hoof marks and scratched in the dirt with his fingers. "Might have realized they're being followed, Hayden. Looks like they've worked themselves up for a run to Texas. Dumb bastards probably think we can't, or won't, follow if they make it to the other side of the Red River. Gonna be in for a hell of a surprise when we catch up with them."

Few hours later, we ran across some of the extra horses they'd been pulling along. The murdering swine had taken one spare each to swap out in the futile hope they could outrun us. 'Bout an hour after that, we found the woman's body. God, but I hated being a prophet when it came to murder, and especially when it came to the mindless slaughter of women. Can't think of anything, in my past, more upsetting than finding the body of a woman mistreated, and then murdered by monsters like Charlie Two Knives or the Crooke brothers.

The brigands killed her near a creek just north of the Wildhorse River. Left the poor girl beside the trail like a pile of discarded trash. She'd curled up with her hands under a battered head, as though she'd just stopped for a minute to get some sleep. All three of us shed some bitter tears over that pitiful corpse.

Billy wiped his eyes with the back of a gloved hand and said, "Damn, Hayden. She might have been a whore, but she didn't deserve to die like this."

Carlton jerked his hat off and swabbed a sweating face with his bandanna. "No woman deserves to die like this, Billy—out in the wild places, far from the safety of family and home. It's a goddamned, sorry shame. And I, for one, aim to see the men what done it pay for the crime with their rotten lives."

Billy flatly refused, so I searched the girl's clothing. Couldn't find any kind of identifying papers on her. No name, nothing that could have helped us determine whose daughter, sister, wife, or mother she might have been.

Took over an hour, and put us even further behind our prey, but we carried rocks from the creek until we'd covered her up with enough to keep the wolves off. Quicker than digging a hole, and about all we could do at the time.

Guess my frustration with the entire murderous chase managed to spill out. Read a selection from *Hamlet* over that poor, unnamed girl's pathetic grave. "This goodly frame, the earth, seems to me a sterile promontory: this most excellent canopy, the air, . . . this brave o'erhanging firmament, this majestical roof fretted with golden fire, why, it appears no other thing to me but a foul and pestilent congregation of vapors. What a piece of wor

is a man! How noble in reason! How infinite in faculty!
In form, in moving, how express and admirable! In action how like an angel! In apprehension how like a god!
And yet, to me, what is this quintessence of dust? Man
delights not me; no, nor woman either. Leave her to
heaven, and to those thorns that in her bosom lodge, to
prick and sting her."

We rode away from that sad place and redoubled our
efforts on the trail. The Two Knives–Crooke brothers'
plan almost worked. Before long, our animals needed a
breather, so we walked every few miles, then rode. Finally, fatigue put us down, animal and man alike. Carlton brought the whole parade to a stop twenty miles
south of the Wildhorse River. We napped for a spell then
hit the trail again. Rode, walked, even ran beside our
animals all night. Held on to the tail of the horse in front
of me, to keep from falling asleep.

Bone weary, about ready to drop, we spotted the outlaw camp right before sunrise. In the middle of a rolling
plain, covered in brittle, knee-deep grass, so dry a single
spark would cause a raging inferno, a lonely stand of
sheltering cottonwoods huddled next to a nameless
creek. Entire site could be seen from a mile away.

Soon as we knew for sure we'd found them, our en-
ergy returned. Trail exhaustion left me like water off a
baby duck's back. Don't ever let anyone tell you any
different, my friends. There's just nothing like the sure-
fire prospect of being shot dead soon to get a man's
juices back up and running fast.

Guess the villains figured we'd given up on catching
them. Only reason I could come up with to make a stab
at understanding some of the things the silly bastards
did. Stupidest of their blunders included going so far as
    build a fire. From half a mile away, the scent of

cooked coffee and country bacon frying led us in by our noses.

Carlton smiled, shook his head, wagged a finger at the trees, and said, "You boys keep on cooking. 'Bout another thirty minutes or so and I'll be eating your bacon, and everyone of you'll be dancin' with the devil."

When our stomachs started grumbling, Billy handed each of us some of the best beef jerky I'd ever put in my mouth. Between chaws, Carlton grinned like a kid at a birthday party and said, "Damn, that's awful good meat, Billy. Why you been holding out on us for so long? We coulda been sucking on this sweet-tastin' stuff ever since we left Antlers."

"Wanted to keep something in reserve, Carlton. This might come as a shock, ole son, but you ain't the best cook in the world. So I always have a stash of this stuff in my war bag, anytime you and I go out together. Woo Chow Pong, Chinese feller who owns that restaurant over on South Phoenix, makes it for me. You know where I'm talking about. Calls it the Trade Winds Cafe. One that has all them red paper lanterns hanging out front."

Carlton closed his eyes like he'd fallen asleep and was dreaming, but kept chewing. "Oh, yeah. I like his place, and that Chinky food he cooks." Then he turned on me. "Well, Hayden, what do you think?"

We'd hidden ourselves in a dry creek bed about five hundred yards from where our band of murderers laid up. Mulled the problem over for a spell before I finally decided to take the situation firmly in hand and put an end to the whole mad mess. The three of us had seen all we wanted of *innocent* bloodshed. Time had come for the Crooke boys, Two Knives, and those running with them to spend eternity in the cold, cold ground.

Way past time for the Brotherhood of Blood to rid the world of the sorry shadows of men not worthy of trial by a jury of their peers or dignified with a well-attended celebratory hanging in Fort Smith.

While my friends checked the loads in their shotguns, rifles, and pistols, I said, "Well, fellers, this looks like the first official skirmish for the Brotherhood. Don't want either of you getting hurt. Take your time, keep your heads down, be careful, and let's get this thing done right. Go in fast. Kill 'em all. Don't let any of the sons of bitches out alive. Even if some manage to survive the assault, you both know what we must do. Hopefully, this passel of scum won't come peaceable. Far as I'm concerned, resistance has always made killing a bad man a whole bunch easier."

"How're we gonna handle it, Hayden?" Billy breached his shotgun and dropped shells into the cut-down twelve-gauge.

I picked up a twig and drew the stand of cottonwoods in the dirt. "Be willing to bet there's a branch of this creek that has some water in it south of the trees. Carl, you make your way to that side. We'll give you a fifteen-minute head start. Billy will go around to the east. I'll come at them from a kind of northwest direction, to close the backdoor on any that might try to get between us when you step in and flush them out. If what Bix told us is accurate, there shouldn't be but four of them left. Of course, that might be nothing more than a guess. Someone could've been waiting for them when they got here. No way to tell right now. Just scare the whole bunch my direction, no matter how many you find. Billy and I'll take care of everything from that point on."

Carlton held his rifle in one hand, a shotgun in the other. "It's a good plan, Hayden," he said. "I know this place. Not much to hide behind, once you get past the brush growing under those trees out front. Mother Nature did the thing, but you'd swear someone planted all them cottonwoods in a nice four-acre circle, right next to the creek. Don't remember any outriders or sheltering hidey-holes, just a pleasant spot to put up for the night, or spend some time out of the sun. Once we got 'em circled, they ain't got a chance in hell of getting away from us."

I pulled the Winchester, levered all the rounds out, and reloaded. Checked to make sure every loop in the top row of my cartridge belt held a rifle shell. Unloaded and reloaded my belly gun and hip pistol. Finally, we kind of nodded at each other, winked, and the Brotherhood of Blood headed out on foot to do what had to be done.

Made it to a piece of broken timber less than a hundred yards from the trees. Spotted Billy as he darted in and out of the grass off to my left. Carlton bled into the landscape like a ghost. Propped my rifle across the log. Hung my hat on a convenient snag. Crouched down and waited for the dance to get started. Took twenty minutes or so before I heard Carlton yell. His voice floated over to me, as clear as a Baptist church bell ringing out for the Sunday-go-to-meeting faithful.

"Charlie Two Knives, Myron Crooke, Byron Crooke, this is Deputy U.S. Marshal Carlton J. Cecil speaking. My fellow deputies and I have warrants for you boys and all those in your company. Lay down your guns. Come out of those trees with your hands above your heads, palms exposed. Give up, right now. You'll be spared and taken in for trial in Fort Smith. If you fight, we intend to kill every damned one of you lice-riddled skunks."

Don't have any idea which one of those thugs said
it, but a voice that sounded like a shot fired from a
Sharps buffalo gun blasted back, "Well, Deputy Marshal
Carlton J. Cecil, you can shit in your hat, fall back in
it, wipe your ass with them warrants, and then you can
go straight to hell." Nervous laughter from several others
followed the smart-mouthed response. "Ain't nobody
here slinking back to Fort Smith so that ugly son of a
bitch George Maledon can stretch his neck with a piece
of oiled Kentucky hemp. Go right ahead and try to take
us, you law-bringing sons of bitches. We'll see all of
you bastards dead as Judas."

'Bout that time, I heard gunfire from Billy's direction.
Another lethal encounter with hot lead and quick death
had begun in earnest.

Couple of fellers came squirting out on my side of
their prairie oasis like a pair of corncrib rats. Loose shirt-
tails fluttered in the haze-laden breeze. Carried their
boots like they'd just woke up and pulled at the reins of
reluctant horses trailing behind. One out front wore a
tall crowned hat with a feather stuck in the band. Over
his loose shirt, he sported a fringed vest covered with
beadwork so brightly rendered, it made me wonder at
the good sense of wearing such an easy-to-spot target.

Didn't take much effort on my part to knock them
down from where I'd set up. Lined my sights on the one
in back first. The .45-70 slug knocked him sideways,
like he'd been hit with a galvanized bucket full of river
rocks. The skittish jarhead mare he lead bolted, headed
back into the trees.

Leader of the pair dropped to one knee and sprayed
pistol fire at anything moving. He didn't have any idea
who had shot his friend, or where the death-dealing blast
me from. At seven and a half inches, the barrel on his

Cavalry-model Colt wasn't much of a match for my Winchester. I let him have three more free ones, then took a bead on that fancy vest, and splattered him out like a dung beetle that'd been stomped on.

Blasting from Carlton's direction flared up and got mighty intense. Sounded like Billy was putting considerable pressure on anyone in front of his pistols. Gunfire from Billy's side of the disagreement moved into the tree line. Folks yelled, horses whinnied and squealed, and the barrage grew more concentrated. Added to all the noise and confusion, for a horrifying instant, could have sworn I heard a woman scream.

Hopped up and ran toward the center of that patch of scruffy trees. Couldn't see much of anything. Scrub brush grew almost chest high, in places, once you got to the outer circle of cottonwoods. Everything fell away to a shade-covered, grassless, bowl-shaped area kept bare by a lack of sunlight. Bottom of the bowl was veined with a web-work of cottonwood roots running on top of the ground in all directions. Always hated that particular characteristic of those trashy trees.

Shouting and shooting slacked off. I crept up to the center of the camp. Several dead horses littered the ground. A couple that had been wounded made considerable noise in their panicked distress. Had to put them out of their misery myself. In the middle of the whole shebang sat a spring wagon. A well-dressed dead man with tied hands and feet decorated the rough wooden seat like a blanket draped over it for comfort. Someone had slashed his throat from ear to ear, and he'd bled out right where he lay.

A badly wounded man had backed up against a huge V-shaped tree, not far from the wagon. He held a pistol to the head of a trembling young woman. Blood drippe from his gun hand onto her shoulder. As he adjusted the arm around her waist, a crazed and crooked grin decorated his filthy face like a picture hung by a five-year-old child. His dying partner slumped against them, scarcely able to hold his bullet-riddled body erect. Useless pistols dangled from limp, barely functioning fingers.

About fifteen feet away, Carlton strode up on one side of the trio, Billy on the other. As I made my way to close the circle, the killer clutching the girl said, "Well, y'all done kilt brother Byron fer damned sure. He cain't but barely stand. The one of you sons of bitches, what done the yelling, shot him full of lead in the first volley. Got near 'bouts a dozen holes in him." He swallowed hard, like a man stranded in the desert, coughed, and spit a gob of blood onto the girl's already saturated shoulder. "I thought Two Knives and Snake Witherspoon wuz hard cases, but if'n you're the only lawdogs around, y'all musta kilt 'em, or some of you would have already lit a shuck and struck out after 'em."

The woman tried to pull away, but he tightened his hold. Surprised the hell out of everyone and almost scared him witless when she screamed, "Kill him. Kill the son of a bitch. Do it now."

Took him a second to regain his composure, but Myron Crooke's arm slid up her body, stopped at her throat. He pulled her head sidewise and, in a hissing voice, said, "Hold still now, Miz Lucy. You wouldn't want me to accidentally blow your pretty brains out, now would you?"

Don't know how she managed, but the woman twisted in his grip and spit right into his open mouth. Then she turned, looked me directly in the eye, and said, clearly and calmly as a mother talking to her child,

"You can shoot through me with that big rifle, Marshal. My father owned a gun like yours, so I know you can do it. After the unspeakable sins committed upon my person by this animal and those other vermin last night, quick death would be a God-sent blessing."

Any color that remained in Myron Crooke's face bled right into his boots. Stunned don't even come close to describing the look left on him when she finished speaking. None of us could believe it, but, in a mocking voice, the nervy bastard said, "Aw, now, Miz Lucy, you know you don't mean that. Hell, things work out right, we might get married someday, being as how your husband died so sudden like."

She spat on him again and snapped, "Then go ahead. Kill me yourself, you soulless bastard. I'd rather be dead than have to spend another second with your hands on me."

Hard to believe, but Myron Crooke, a man responsible for the murders of six or seven people actually appeared hurt by what she'd said. When his brother Byron flopped out on the ground at his feet, right in front of him, and drew a last bloody, gurgling breath, the man looked downright pitiful.

His gaze came up from his dead brother's face, and swept back and forth over the three of us as he said, "We warn't bad men, you know. It were the whiskey what done it. Rotten stuff burned Byron's pea-sized brain completely away. Tried to stop him, but after he'd kilt Mary Beth Tall Dog, well, the boy just went crazier'n a sackful of sun-struck lizards. Course once he got the game started, have to admit, I jumped right in and went along for the ride. But good God, when he painted them fellers up in that tent saloon, after he kilt 'em, it really got to me. Tried to stop him after that mess of murders. But goddammit, I weren't able to do no good." Honest to God, ole Myron acted like he was gonna break down and cry like a baby.

He leaned heavily against the cottonwood and closed his eyes. For about a second, I thought the whole affair might end with him turning the girl loose and giving up. Just goes to show how good I was about predicting human behavior. Good thing no one had me on payroll for such worthless thoughts.

All of a sudden, his eyes snapped open, and with a voice that sounded like it came from the bottom of a newly dug grave, he said, "Good God, but I'm sure glad my dear ole mama ain't still alive. Finding out about this would've surely kilt her." He pulled the trigger, and the blast knocked poor Miz Lucy three feet.

Hammer on his pistol barely had time to strike the cap, when Billy Bird's right hand came up filled with one of those big Schofield .45s. It delivered a monster slug that hit Myron Crooke just below his right eye. Sent him on an express ride straight to hell. The hand holding his pistol disappeared in a red vaporous mist at the same instant the load from Carlton's shotgun blew a cavern in his chest. Several rounds from my Winchester nailed him to the tree, for about five seconds, before he crumpled to the ground like an emptied-out corn-husk doll. His limp corpse dropped across the legs of his already departed moonstruck loon of a brother.

Wouldn't have thought of stopping him anyway, but Billy surprised me a bit when he jumped over to the rapidly cooling carcass of little brother Byron and put two quick ones in the dead boy's skull. Then he twirled his pistol on his finger, dropped it into the holster, and said, "Don't know about you boys, but I feel much better now. Folks all over the Nations can sleep tonight, and not have to worry about being murdered by these sons of bitches."

Carlton kneeled over Miz Lucy and called out, "Get over here, Hayden. This lady's still alive."

Hard to believe, but ole Myron's hand must have shook at just the right moment, or could have been she ducked a split second before he pulled the trigger. Either way, his errant shot had burned a deep crease across the base of her skull, but left everything else pretty much undamaged and intact.

Once we'd mopped her down with some cool creek water and she started to come around, Carlton smiled like the village idiot. Think he was the happiest man in the Nations right then. Emotion almost overcame us all. After so much blood and death, we'd actually pulled someone back from the threshold of eternity.

Don't know exactly why, not any real way to explain such things, but she latched on to Billy Bird like a person drowning. Maybe the female instinct just naturally recognized the only one of us that wasn't attached. Then again, guess it could've been, for the first time in his life, the woman who'd always been out there looking for the boy had finally appeared. Whatever the cause, I noticed it was the only existing instance, in my memory, when Billy Bird seemed totally at ease around a real, actual female-type person. While Carlton and I worked like field hands, cleaning up the mess of dead men and animals, Billy stayed with the devastated woman and, in pretty short order, had her back around to something close to normalcy.

Later that night, Lucy sat next to a fire that contained Billy's almost worn-out shovel. With his best blanket draped over her shoulders, she told a dreadful tale of murder and insanity. "My husband, Harold Waggone and I simply made the wrong decision at the worst possible time. We'd been to visit my relatives in Pine Bluff, Arkansas, and were on our way back to Wichita Falls when we stopped here to rest three days ago. It's a beautiful and pleasant spot. We have enjoyed stops here on several previous trips. Shaded and cool most afternoons, you know. We had a nice breeze pass early yesterday morning. At certain times of the year, the fragrance of prairie wildflowers drifts in and is most gratifying."

She hesitated a moment. Gazed at the stars blinking between the dense cover of tree limbs and sighed. "Two Knives and his monsters arrived about midday. Waltzed into camp bristling with pistols and knives. They trussed Harold up like a Christmas turkey and took turns having their way with me for the rest of the night."

That simple rendition of the facts seemed to suck the life right out of her. For a few seconds, I thought she might not be able to go on with her recitation of murder and madness, but she took a deep breath and waded right back in. "I didn't know those animals had killed Harold till this morning, when they dragged me out of that patch of bushes over there and made me start breakfast."

She took a sip of coffee, then brushed an errant strand of ebony hair out of her face. "I'm pretty sure the brute they called Snake Witherspoon was the one who murdered my husband. He bragged of the deed when he took me again, after the others tired out. I could think of no reason, at the time, not to believe him."

Guess she'd said all she wanted, or was capable of telling us. Know for damned sure, if what happened to Mrs. Waggoner had been visited on me, I might never have been able to tell it. As a matter of course, over the years I've noticed when it comes to such abhorrent occurrences, women tend to be much stronger than men.

From my friend Missy Talbot to Lucy Waggoner, the women have always seemed able to adjust to such treatment better than any man of my acquaintance. Unfortunately, bad men generally kept an overheated eye out for any available female. Once those animals satisfied their most primitive urges, the poor women usually met with tragic and brutal ends. Those females who survived tapped into a well of character far deeper than most of us hairy-legged types could ever lay a claim on.

"Would you like one of us to accompany you to your home in Wichita Falls, Mrs. Waggoner?" Carlton's question broke the silence and seemed to bring her back to reality, away from the edges of mental exhaustion.

She thought about his query for some moments before saying, "No, I have no wish to go there. My home and family are in Arkansas. Now that Harold's gone, there's nothing left for me in Texas."

Billy said, "Well, that settles it. You can come to Fort Smith with us. If you wish to continue on to your family's home in Arkansas, I'll see you arrive safely." He smiled, refilled her cup, put the coffeepot back on the fire, then gently adjusted the blanket over her shoulders.

Before we covered those murderin' skunks with dirt, I inked the palm of each dead desperado, and pressed it to the back of a John Doe warrant. The judge and his private bailiff, Mr. Wilton, still required the documents as proof of my having dispatched men I believed beyond the pale of justice. Two Knives and the Crooke boys fit that category better than any I'd come across in quite a spell.

We started our return to civilization the following morning. Lucy Waggoner improved with every step. She'd placed wildflowers on the grave of her husband before we began the trek, and that simple act seemed to bring the whole tragedy to a close. In those bloody, desperate days, everyone lived so intimately with death, such events had to be left behind as quickly as possible.

The more distance we put between ourselves and the horrors we'd left in the wake of our search, the better we all felt. Seriously considered going back to Atoka and catching the train, but decided against it. Realized how close Billy and Lucy were becoming with each minute they spent together. Don't get me wrong here. None of what happened cast any reflection on the memory of Lucy's poor dead husband. But, he was dead, and she had to move on with her life.

13

"YOU COULD NOT HAVE PREVENTED THIS"

BY THE TIME the Arkansas River's muddy face finally roiled into view, I think all of us had actually pushed most of the horror from the previous few weeks into a part of our hearts and minds where the ghastly events no longer had to be revisited. May seem a bit on the gruesome side, to most modern sensibilities, but there was a time when folks knew for damned sure that living caused dying, and death was an ever-present, elbow-to-elbow companion who couldn't wait to wrap his bony, life-ending fingers tightly around your heart.

We had pulled up on the Nations side of the river when I spotted my trusted friend, Daniel Old Bear. Long gray hair flitted around his slumped shoulders and danced to a tune only he could hear. On his favorite blanket, he sat under a tree near the ferry slips, leaned slightly to one side, rested his free hand across Caesar's back, and puffed on a corncob pipe. Tobacco smoke twisted and swirled above his head. The dog quietly slept. Glad to see my errant companion had made it back home to our mutual friend. The yellow-haired beast had vanished just after we found the Homer Richland party burned up and hanging in the trees near the Washita.

I never worried much about Caesar's well-being. The huge creature always came, and went, as he pleased. Just like Old Bear. They both enjoyed a kind of independence most of us would have given anything to possess. Appeared when they wanted, stayed as long as they cared to, and departed only to turn up again when most needed.

Knew as soon as I saw him that Old Bear hadn't materialized on the banks of the Arkansas to bring me good tidings. He stood as I approached and exhibited the look of a man carrying a full load of bad news. A map of pain like a set of Missouri, Kansas, and Texas Railroad tracks etched itself across his forehead and around his eyes.

Climbed down and shook the hand he offered. He gently placed a steadying one on my shoulder and said, "Glad to see you my old friend. Caesar and I've been awaiting your arrival for about a week. Elizabeth sent us." Then, he said the words every man living fears more than all others. "I'm afraid something awful has occurred, Hayden. You're needed at home as quickly as we can get there."

Don't know what Old Bear told them, but each of my clearly concerned friends shook my hand, before I departed, and said he'd be along later. Lucy Waggoner kissed my cheek and whispered, "Thank you, Marshal ̄ilden. I owe my life to you, and your friends." We waved ourselves away from Carlton, Billy, and the new widow at the courthouse, then fogged it for my home out on the Arkansas, north of town.

Daniel escorted me through Fort Smith. Once we'd cleared city streets, we kicked toward Van Buren, as fast as good horses could run. My friend didn't utter another word about his "something awful" until we were less than half a mile away, and I could see the house. He'd said Elizabeth sent him, so it just naturally followed in my mind that she was still alive, and something else must be amiss.

For some reason, the notion that perhaps our home had burned grabbed me, and wouldn't turn loose until the house came fully into view. Fires were an all-too-common occurrence in those days. Unfortunately, once a blaze got started it usually consumed everything its scorching tongue touched. We lived so far out of town, Fort Smith's company of volunteer firefighters couldn't have done much good, even if they'd managed to show up. My closest neighbor's house had caught fire the year before and been reduced to a pile of charcoal in a matter of a few blazing minutes. Hard experience taught me that trying to put out a fire with buckets always proved a futile proposition and a total waste of effort. Might as well try to dampen the embers of hell with a thimble.

No obvious damage to the house was in evidence with the naked eye, but a number of horses and carriages stood in the yard. One of them, a fancy black rig, belonged to Judge Parker. I knew then, beyond any doubt, something more serious than I had guessed must have occurred.

With less than five hundred yards to go, we pulled up and slowed our animals to a quick trot. Old B⋅ turned to me and said, "Young Tommy came down the putrid throat two weeks ago. Most terrible case I've ever seen, Hayden. Indian or white, this one was the worst. Boy didn't have any more chance than a snow-flake in July of surviving. We did everything we could. Doc Wheeler swabbed the boy's tonsils, and such, with tincture of iodine and nitrate of silver. He even tried several other remedies, but nothing helped. I built a sweat lodge out back of the house and boiled pine tar for the child to inhale. Didn't work. The demon took hold, and little Tommy went down quick. You've ar-rived just in time for the boy's funeral."

Diphtheria—every parent's worst nightmare. No known cure at the time. Lots of absolutely torturous folk remedies around, but almost twenty years would come and go before the method for saving my son finally ap-peared and enjoyed common use. Poor child was just born in the wrong place and time to stay with us any longer than he did.

Don't think I could have been more shocked by Dan-iel's news if the worm-riddled corpse of Saginaw Bob had popped out of the road bed right in front of me and said, "See, Tilden, you and all them other shit-kickers thought you'd done got rid of me, when Maledon stretched my neck for killin' off your entire family in '79. But hell, bubba, I'm back and ready to rub out as many as I can while I'm around."

For unfathomable reasons, the thought that my son might die before me had never entered my mind. In spite of the brutality and unknowable dangers of my work, I'd planned on living a long life—the end of which would be filled with children, grandchildren, and fond memories of the early, hard times. Fully expected to go my own grave with Tommy, and his extensive family, hing the service, singing hymns, and weeping over the loss of *Grandpa* Tilden. I had secretly entertained daydreams of a granddaughter who would look exactly like Elizabeth. Guess it's the same with all fathers. We do tend to dream great dreams of the future for our children.

Elizabeth met Daniel and me at the door. She fell on my chest in a blond-haired, blue-eyed avalanche of tears and grief. Judge Parker, and Carlton's wife, Judith, stood behind her with comforting hands on each of her shoulders, as if to keep her from falling to the floor in a helpless heap at my feet. Don't think I could have helped her up if she had collapsed. I felt like a ghost in my own house. I've heard folks tell as how certain events caused them to go into a state of disbelief that brought on a feeling of otherworldliness. Seems that's what happened to me.

Good friends, and people I'd never seen before, gathered around us. Dusty deputy marshals fresh off the trail of bad men, clerks who worked in Elizabeth's store, well-dressed businessmen from all over town, their weeping wives, and untold numbers of church folk expressed heartfelt condolences. Each offered all manner of personal assistance and comfort in what most of them referred to as "our time of tragedy and great loss." A good many concerned friends stood in the privacy of various corners and appeared to be praying.

My teary-eyed wife held a lace handkerchief over her raw, reddened nose and led me into the parlor. Tucked into the niche of our bay window, surrounded by a virtual garden of cut flowers, a tiny, gold-trimmed casket sat on a black draped platform. Light streamed into the room from a window behind the arrangement. Radiated heat, generated by those sunbeams, heightened the combined fragrances from an amazing array of bloom plants. A single, dancing luminous streak caressed our dead son's face as if God himself had just visited and left a smiling kiss on the cheeks of a child who still appeared to be living.

I put my arm around Elizabeth's quaking shoulders and reached into the coffin to hold Tommy's icy little hand. "It all happened so quickly, Hayden," she mumbled into my shoulder. "There are a number of others also. Doc Wheeler is afraid we might be on the verge of an epidemic."

An unavoidable feeling of profound guilt washed over me like Mississippi floodwaters and almost brought me to my knees. Somehow Elizabeth guessed my feelings. She forced herself against me as if to prop me up and keep me from falling. She whispered, "It wasn't your fault, dearest Hayden. You could not have prevented this. Once the contagion took hold, everything that could possibly have been done was done."

But remorse and grief have always combined to form a damnedly tough hill to climb. I kissed the tears from her cheeks and said, "Just wish I had managed to get back home sooner. I would like to have held him in my arms for the last few hours of his short life. Perhaps he could have drawn enough strength from me to survive. I would've willingly given up as many years of my life, as necessary, to save his."

She caressed my arm. "No, Hayden. Families all over Arkansas are going to lose children to this calamity. Any youngster spared will count himself among the luckiest alive in the years to come."

We never knew exactly how he'd managed to conract the infection. But looking back today, the sickness ─bably came to him from children he played with, ─ visiting his mother at the store. No one fully understood how the ailment got spread in those days. I decided Elizabeth was right. Punishing yourself for ignorance, or the undone deeds of the past, is a total waste of time. You just have to play the hand as dealt, hope for the best, and keep your eye on the future.

And so, on a small, oak-shaded hill, just west of the main house, we buried Thomas Jefferson Tilden boy, next day. That tiny plot of dirt, encircled by a waist-high fence of hammered iron, eventually held my entire family—all nineteen of them. Lost some to other childhood diseases, some to accidents, but most to the great influenza epidemic of 1918. Still find it most appalling to remember how many people went to Jesus on that wave of death. To this very moment, can't imagine a single reason why I survived. Hardest of all, the pestilence even took Elizabeth.

Our closest friends attended Tommy's sad little service. Carlton and his wife, Judith, along with Billy Bird, Lucy Waggoner, and Old Bear, stood directly behind Elizabeth and me in a show of love and support money can't buy. Judge Parker, his wife, and his two sons were present. Mr. and Mrs. Wilton, and their brood of seven, came to show their respects—along with a host of others too large to list. All together, Elizabeth and I took part in more than thirty funerals that winter.

Once, for just about a second when the clods had started to fall on the boy's coffin, I glanced away from the open grave and the tiny tombstone protected on each side by marble angels. God as my witness, I saw Handsome Harry Tate standing on the front steps of my house. Dressed in a fine-looking suit, he held his hat in nervous hands and waved when he noticed me watching.

I'd be willing to swear on a stack of Bibles I heard Harry say, "It's fine, Hayden. Tommy's with me, a we're just fine as frog hair. You needn't worry."

Chills ran up and down my sweaty spine. Gooseflesh rippled all over my arms and chest. I'd never held any beliefs concerning ghosts, till that sad afternoon. Often had dreams about those who'd passed on. At times, the dearly departed came to me with advice in my nightly reveries, still do. But I'd never seen anyone positively known to be among the dead walking around in broad daylight like Harry. Leastways, not till that heartbreaking morning. From then on, I held the position of a true believer. Had to. No other way to explain it.

Bad news didn't stop with Tommy's funeral. Heard sometime later as how Precious Tall Dog never recovered from her ordeal. Story that came to me allowed as how she'd made up her mind not to live any longer, and didn't. Mighty sad ending for a child so beautiful. Hit Dennis Limber Hand so hard he killed himself. Only instance of such behavior by an Indian feller I'd ever heard of. Retaught me a hard lesson. Blood tended to beget more blood. Murder, rape, and death spread out from the Crooke brothers like ripples in a lethal pond. All brought on by a mess of bad whiskey and weak-minded men.

These days, the numberless departed of my long life seem to visit me on a fairly regular basis. Beginning to think I might have to install signs at the foot of my bed, at Rolling Hills, to control the traffic of the long deceased and sometimes forgotten. Might not be a bad idea to charge a toll. Beginning to think I'd get rich.

It took a number of years for Elizabeth and me to completely recover from my first son's death. We both poured ourselves back into our work with a vengeance. She bought a bank in Siloam Springs. The travel seemed help her deal with the loss. And, like everything else she touched, her new bank turned into another huge pile of money so fast I couldn't believe it. About a year later, my daughter Dianna made her appearance. Thanks to a gracious God, she looked almost exactly like her mother. Dianna's birth helped considerably, but I still spent too much time out by Tommy's grave, when back from my latest raid in the Nations.

'Bout once a year, Elizabeth would hug me close and say something like, "You know, you don't have to squander your time chasing killers anymore, Hayden. We've got more money than any ten of the best Arkansas families could spend in two lifetimes." Just her gentle reminder that I could stay home, if that's what I wanted.

Hell, near as I could tell, Elizabeth didn't care if I sat on the veranda all day long staring at the Arkansas, with Caesar warming my feet, and never hit another lick at anything resembling work again. Course, being a man, I was naturally inclined toward life as a professional layabout. So I seriously thought her offer over, more than once.

But chasing killers, villains, and other evildoers was all I knew. Didn't want to start pushing a plow again; besides, the Brotherhood of Blood had only begun in its quest to rid the world of monsters. There's lot worse ways of spending your time than bringing bad men to justice. Mine was the life of the lawdog, and I knew in the secret recesses of my hidden heart, nothing would change till my tired, bullet-riddled, busted-up ole body just couldn't make the chase anymore, or someone like the Crooke brothers put me in an early grave beside my son.

14

"FOUND HER UNCLOTHED BODY UNDER A BUSH"

A THOUGHTFUL SILENCE descended on big-time movie producer A. Maxwell Vought's favorite table at the Brown Derby restaurant. The noisy noontime crowd of martini tipplers had departed and left us pretty much to ourselves. Vought sat slumped in a gaudy, over-stuffed, brocaded dining chair, his chin resting in a cupped hand. Lisette and Victoria sniffled into their nap-kins, and Heddy caressed my arm as if to reassure me I could still count myself with the living, and that she cared deeply for my welfare—even if no one else did—a most generous and comforting gesture on her part. Made me love the girl even more.

For some moments no one stirred. Vought finally sat up, leaned with his elbows on the table again, and said, "Well, Hayden, ole buddy, that's one hell of a story.

But, I think we'll have to give the bloody tale some serious consideration, and get back to you later. I'm not sure present-day audiences are quite ready for such an unvarnished dose of reality—perhaps a few years down the road. I've heard serious rumors of a hard-as-nails script about a town marshal who has to face a bunch of killers that come to town on the noonday train. Maybe if someone actually makes it, we can give some serious thought about the Brotherhood of Blood. You and Lightfoot go ahead, cook me up a treatment, and I'll option the idea. 'Bout the best I can do right now."

Well, that kinda brought the whole shootin' match to an abrupt close. Everyone jumped out of his, or her, seat, shook my hand, and thanked me for coming. Lisette and Victoria smiled and kissed my leathery cheeks. All said, they'd had a hell of a ride and enjoyed every minute of it, then hustled out. Hey, I understood. Nothing personal, you know, just business as usual—other places to go, other people to see, and other irons in the fire.

Next day, Alfonso drove Lightfoot, Heddy, and me to some dark, wood-paneled law offices on Wilshire Boulevard. Junior and me signed a contract that granted Vought the right to make a movie about my life based on the boy's *Lawdog* newspaper articles and the book. Split that big pile of money right down the middle. I gave Heddy five thousand dollars. Girl hugged my neck and cried like a baby.

Went from those sterile offices straight out to the airport. Alfonso helped me onto the plane and got me seated. He shook my hand. Handed me a box wrapped in Los Angeles newspapers. Leaned over and whispered, "It's a bottle of the finest tequila made, Señor Tilden. From my hometown in Mexico." He pronounced it Me-hi-co. "Legend says, you drink the whole thing, amigo, eat the worm in the bottom, and you'll see God."

"First chance I get, Alfonso, I'll try that one out. Acquainted with *mucho* folks who claim to know God, but haven't had the distinct pleasure of meeting Him yet myself."

He flashed me a toothy smile. "It has been my great pleasure to know you, Señor. I'll not soon forget our trip to the Santa Monica Pier. *Vaya con Dios, mi amigo viejo.*"

"*Hasta luego,* Alfonso." Course I knew I'd never see him again, but that was just about all the Spanish I could lay my poor old tongue on.

Don't remember much about the trip back. By then, I'd pretty much worn myself out. Think I slept all the way from Dallas to Little Rock on the train. Took me damned near a month to recover from the whole shooting match. One of the nicer results of the expedition was the way Chief Nurse Leona Wildbank acted when I got back. Swear to God, for just about a second or so, thought that big ole gal was gonna break right down and shed a tear or two. But she held 'em back. Don't know exactly what happened, but, from then on, she pretty much left sweet little Heddy McDonald and me on our own.

Late one night, about a month after we got back, I couldn't sleep. Typical old man shit. Aches here, pains there, too many things whizzing through my ancient brain. Took Alfonso's bottle of cactus juice and snuck out to the sun porch. General Black Jack Pershing hopped up in my lap, and snuggled his yellow-striped self down into the leg comforter Heddy knitted for me.

The cat and me smoked us a cigar and drank that whole bottle of tequila. Wasn't really a full-sized fifth, you know. Must have been some kind of Mexican liquor measurement. Looked about three-quarters the size of a regular bottle of hooch. Maybe it was a pint. No, more than that. Anyhow, took me about an hour to finally kill it off.

When we hit the bottom of the bottle, I sucked Alfonso's magic worm out and chewed its rubbery ass up just like a piece of left over corkscrew macaroni from Rolling Hill's lunchroom. With God as my witness, 'bout ten minutes later, Carlton J. Cecil strolled in big as life and twice as obnoxious. Looked like he did the first time we met—tall, thin, red-haired, and stringy muscled—young again. Had his hat pushed onto the back of his head and wore three pistols. Silver Mexican rowels sparkled, chinked, and sang as he sauntered over to my chair. Ghost grinned like a henhouse fox that'd just sucked every egg in the place dry as a bone. Damned impressive for a dead man I'd cremated and personally tossed into the Arkansas River.

Snatched the bottle out of my hand and turned it straight up. Then, pointed his finger in my face and said, "Hell, that's just like you not to save me any, Tilden. Damned dry over here where I am." Dropped the bottle in my lap and strolled over to the window. Sat down on the sill, rolled a smoke, and puffed away like a sawmill chimney.

"Thought you was gonna tell it all, Tilden. That's what we agreed on, warn't it?"

"Just a damned minute, old man. I never agreed to anything. You're the one who said we should tell it all. Remember?"

"Who the hell you calling an old man? Over here on this side, there ain't no old people. None of them damned wheelchairs or sorry-assed cafeteria food. No colostomy bags or any of that kind of medieval shit.

Hell, me and my good friend Barnes Reed can have a pie-eating contest every day, if'n we want to. Fact is, I got up from the table at the Napoli Cafe just especially to come down here to talk to you, you old fart. Ate six chocolate pies, in one sitting. Barnes is still bangin' on the table and a-laughin' his head off."

"What've you got to talk to me about that would get you away from heaven, Barnes Reed, and big sugary gobs of toasted meringue?"

"Well, lately I've been thinking a lot about the time I caught Kelp Caldwell. Remember him?"

"Vaguely. We ran a lot of men down during our day, Carlton. Truth is, but don't tell Lightfoot I said this, if push came to shove, I might be able to bring back about half of all the evil bastards we snatched up by the roots. Course I keep telling Franklin J. Lightfoot Junior I can remember everything since the invention of dirt, so don't you go giving me away."

"You gotta remember Caldwell, Tilden. Good-looking feller. All the ladies just thought ole Kelp was about the most handsome man in the Nations. Said he had the best-looking head of hair God ever put on a man, and the face of a Greek statue. Soiled doves in town said he packed a pair of pants better than any man in Arkansas, Texas, Louisiana, or the Nations. Near as anyone could tell, he had his pick of 'em. Heard more than one say ole Kelp could have her just any ole time he wanted. Think most of 'em meant that in the for-damned-sure literal, and biblical, sense."

For some reason a flash of recognition darted through my alcohol-numbed brain. "Ah, you mean the one who killed Lorena London. Hadn't thought about him, or her, in years. God Almighty, but Lorena was one handsome young woman. And as pure as the wind-driven snow, if memory serves."

"That's it, that's the one. Goes back a ways. Back before we started the Brotherhood. Anyhow, she came up missing, and her mother reported the disappearance the same day. Said the girl wasn't given to running away, and such Lady wept the whole time I talked with her. Think she knew what the outcome was gonna be, before I ever put a foot in a stirrup."

People of my acquaintance have claimed that cats can see ghosts. Don't know whether Black Jack could see Carlton and just got tired of the conversation, or if, maybe, he decided I'd gone crazy and figured it was time to take a hike. Whatever came over the fuzzy beast, he jumped off my lap, sashayed down the hall to the nurse's station, and left Carlton's ghost and me to our ramblings.

"You found the poor girl's body, didn't you, Carl?"

"Yeah. That I did." A great sadness seeped into his voice as he continued. "Guess it was 'bout a year after they started sparkin', when Caldwell lured her away from home with the promise of a picnic out on a creek, just off the Arkansas, not all that far from her parents home near Van Buren. Seems he'd been after the girl right strong the whole time. Tried everything in his considerable power to separate her from her female innocence. None of his overheated enticements had worked— must've been a mighty frustrated man. Took some looking, but I found the spot where Miss Lorena'd spent considerable time weaving fresh blooming wildflowers into a garland. You would have had to search a spell to come on a more beautiful place for young lovers to dally on a summer afternoon."

My vision, spirit, or whatever you want to call him

dropped his head, and for a moment looked lost. Then
he said, "I've always felt Caldwell probably let her get
good and comfortable, before he jumped her like a wild
animal and did as he pleased. Near as I could tell, he
didn't kill her right after. Maybe he went back for another helping, or two, before his fatal decision got made.
Don't matter much when he stepped over the last line,
but he did. Drowned that beautiful young girl in about
a foot of water, less than fifty feet from where she'd
picked those wildflowers. I found her unclothed body
under a bush nearby. Dressed her myself, so her mother
wouldn't have to see what I'd seen."

"Jesus, Carl, don't know why, but guess I never really
knew the details of Miss Lorena's sad departure. Know
I heard about the killing, must have forgotten the facts
over the years."

"Yeah. Know what you mean. Well, after I got the
poor girl's body back home to her mother, I tracked that
lowdown murderin' son of a bitch to Anson McMahon's
farm, over near Thackerville."

"That's way down in the Choctaw Nation within spit-
ing distance of Texas, isn't it?"

"Damn right. Took me almost a month to find the
slimy weasel. Rode up to the farm and kinda checked
out the lay of things. Discovered the rumors I'd heard
about Kelp were true. Seems he never got more than
arm's length from a big ole Winchester, kinda like that
one of yours. Wore it across his back, on a thick hand-
tooled leather strap. Was considered by most folks who
knew him as a dead shot and meaner'n a teased rattler,
when trapped. Can you imagine trying to do farm work
with a rifle strapped on your back all day long?"

"Didn't want to get into a gunfight with him, huh?"

"Nope. I wanted his sorry, woman-killing ass alive.

Wanted to watch his face when Judge Parker sentenced him to hang, and take as much pleasure as possible from seeing him kick for hell, after ole Maledon dropped the trap on his arrogant self. Wanted to see the end of his vanity when he messed himself at the end of a piece of oiled Kentucky hemp. Wanted all that for me, Lorena, and the girl's poor distraught mother."

"Always knew you were a hard case, Carlton. Just don't think I ever truly acknowledged your capability for coolly conscious cruelty, or the depths of hatred you could muster up for someone like Kelp Caldwell."

"I didn't hate the evil bastard, Hayden. Just wanted to make damned sure he paid with his life for what he'd done to a beautiful, trusting young woman."

"So, what happened after you got to the farm?"

"No one there knew me, so I did my old drunk, looking-for-work act, and got me a job making three dollars a month, right there beside the son of a bitch. Just to make him more comfortable, took all my guns, except a little Hopkins and Allen .32-caliber hideout revolver, and hung them on a peg inside the kitchen door, where everybody there could see them. Kept the .32 in my left boot. Hell, we bunked up right next to each other in the barn that whole time. Sat beside him when we ate our meals. 'Fore long he got to telling me his life story, bragged 'bout all the things he'd done in the past. Ole Kelp took considerable pride in being a 'bad' man."

"How long did it take you to finally bring him down?"

"Three miserable, chickenshit shoveling weeks. But it only took a few days to discover that a man can really grow to hate a long-handled shovel, in a matter of hours, if he really puts his back to it. Never spent another minute out of another day doin' farm work, after my short stay on Anson McMahon's place."

"Took that long for the right opportunity to come up?"

"Yeah. Fact is I'd about given up on the thing, 'cause Kelp was one spooky wretch. Walked up on him in a freshly plowed field one afternoon. Was about to pull my hideout gun, when he twirled around and snapped that rifle off his back. Had me covered so quick I almost passed out. But then he said, 'Damn, you skeered me some. Didn't realize it was only you, my friend.' All I could do was smile, and get right beside him with my hoe, and go back to work."

"How'd you finally jerk him up short?"

"Few days after that startling episode out in the fields, we were cleaning up for supper. Hired help only had a single basin of water outside the door of Mrs. McMahon's kitchen. For reason's I've never understood, and Caldwell couldn't explain, he took the rifle off, and stood it against the wall a few feet away while he washed up. He'd never done such a careless thing before. When he reached for the towel and buried his wet face in it, I grabbed the Winchester. Soon's he looked up and saw the open muzzle of his own weapon pointed at his heart, he knew exactly what had come down."

"No argument? No fight? He simply gave it up?"

"Yep. I called McMahon outside, and had him put the cuffs on Kelp, while I kept the heartless killer covered. Murderin' scum never said a word. Honest to God, Hayden, he looked me in the eye and all the air kind of gushed out of him. Man knew he was starin' into the face of his own death. Think I felt better, right then, than I had in years."

"But, Carlton, I don't remember anyone named Kelp Caldwell stepping up to Maledon's Gates of Hell gallows."

"That's because he never made it back to Fort Smith. Turned my back on the egg-sucking dog, for ten seconds, about twenty miles southwest of town. He started running, and I started shooting. Killed the son of a bitch with his own rifle. When I got to him, he still had some life left. Said he wanted to thank me for being a good shot. Just couldn't stand the thought of getting strung up. So, I plugged him again. Figured if being shot once made him that happy, another one would send him to meet Satan in a state of sheer ecstasy. Felt compelled to oblige the three-tailed skunk."

"How come you never told me this tale when you was alive? Why'd you have to show up in a vision for me to hear all this?"

He snuffed the cigarette with his thumb and forefinger, placed the butt in his vest pocket, and chinked his way over to a few feet from my chair. "You've probably heard it all somewhere. Just forgot. Wanted to remind you as how we did damned good work, Hayden. In spite of everything, we did damned good work."

"What do you mean by in spite of everything?"

He moved closer, and I'm almost certain I could smell those lemon drops he liked to suck on. "Well, sometimes no matter what we managed to accomplish, things didn't pan out exactly the way we would have liked. See, I stopped over at the London house and was gonna tell Lorena's mother that she could rest easy, 'cause I'd put Caldwell in the ground. Unfortunate woman had lost her mind. Sat in the corner and blubbered all the time. She'd gone nuttier than my grandma Mathilda's Christmas fruitcake. Heard later her poor dis traught husband had to send her to the state hospital over in Little Rock. Never recovered. Died in the crazy house. Hell of a way to go. Still and all, Caldwell paid the price for his pleasures, and I was damned glad to be the one what collected the debt."

Thought the visitation had come to an end. The specter started for the door, and I closed my eyes. Almost as a whisper I heard, "The Brotherhood was the best thing we ever did, Tilden. Don't ever let anyone try to persuade you otherwise. Now that you've let that big, hairy cat out of the bag, tell it all. Even the worst of it."

Woke up and snapped my head toward the door— nothing there. Not a soul in sight. Just an empty hallway. But I swear the smell of lemon drops still lingered in the air. Along with words that kept ricocheting around in my brain. "Tell it all. Even the worst of it." Worst of it could be pretty bad. Texas Ranger Lucius Dodge called it "the grim work of good men."

That's what it was for damned sure. Grim work. Guess I'm gonna have to tell Franklin J. Lightfoot Jr. all about Colonel Cotton Rix. Couldn't get much worse than Cotton, or that bunch of bloodletters of his. Carlton knew 'bout Cotton and how bad that whole affair turned out. He went with me for that round of gun smoke and death, too. Guess I'll have to start Junior on it tomorrow.

But right now, think I'll stroll back down to my room, crawl into my bed, and see if I can get some sleep. Beautiful Heddy should wake me up about seven. Hope Junior waits till sometime after noon to stop in for a visit. Ole Bony Fingers hit the nail on the head. 'on't think I've got but maybe one more fingernail keeping me over here with the living. But, hey, it's a tough one. Before it snaps off I've got a lot more to tell Franklin J. Lightfoot Jr. and all his *Arkansas Gazette* readers.

EPILOGUE

A BOATLOAD OF evil men went to George Maledon's Gates of Hell gallows in Fort Smith as the result of murder done while under the influence of a bucketful of bad liquor. Poor bastards bought the brain-melting rot from lowlife scum too evil to breathe.

Judge Parker had not a lick of tolerance for whiskey peddlers. He believed those who introduced firewater, rotgut, pissin' liquor, or Choctaw beer to the residents of the Nations should expect the harshest kind of lawful punishment when dragged before his widely famed bar of justice. In spite of everything our band of dedicated man-chasing deputy marshals could do, though, illegal scamper juice flowed like rainwater.

Personally, found myself lined up right beside the judge. Always despised drunks of every sort—white, black or Indian. Far as I'm concerned, the inebriate's lack of self-control ranks as the chief of all sins. To this very day, at the doorway to my ninetieth year, still don't have any use for, or patience with, the whiskey-crazed bastards. Their unpredictability, added to slovenly and depraved behavior, always made them dangerous in the extreme.

Only good thing I ever saw come from the bottom of a whiskey jug was the Brotherhood of Blood. It lasted damn near forty years. Good men doin' grim work. I'm proud as hell to have been a small part of it.

J. Lee Butts left the teaching profession in 1981 to seek a career with IBM in Los Angeles, California. After six years with Big Blue managing customer relations for MGM, 20th Century Fox, Orion, William Morris Agency, and other large entertainment accounts, he left the company and worked for a time in the public sector.

Jimmy attends weekly meetings of the DFW Writer's Workshop. His previous Berkley novels are *Lawdog* and *Hell in the Nations*. Other works include nonfiction titles and short pieces for various magazines and reviews. Butts now makes his home in Dallas, Texas.

LINGO BARNES IS ON HIS WAY TO DURANGO,
COLORADO, WHEN HE STUMBLES UPON THE KIDNAPPING
OF EMILY LOU COLTER. NOW HE MUST SAVE THE GIRL
AND KEEP HIMSELF OUT OF THE LINE OF FIRE.

JUSTICE HAS A NEW HOME.

HANGING VALLEY

No one knows the American West better than

JACK BALLAS

Author of *West of the River*

0-425-18410-2

BERKLEY

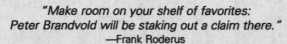

WOLF MACKENNA

THE BURNING TRAIL
0-425-18694-6
"COMPELLING WESTERN WITH FAST ACTION
AND ENGAGING CHARACTERS."
—PETER BRANDVOLD

DUST RIDERS
0-425-17698-3
A VENGEFUL COWBOY AND A TENDERFOOT YANKEE
JOIN FORCES TO TRACK MURDEROUS THIEVES
THROUGH TERRAIN THAT'S EQUALLY DEADLY.

GUNNING FOR REGRET
0-425-17880-3
SHERIFF DIX GRANGER AND HIS PRISONER FIND
THEMSELVES IN THE TOWN OF REGRET, WAITING OUT A
STORM. WHEN ONE OF THE TOWN'S RESIDENTS
KILLS AN APACHE, DIX KNOWS IT'S UP TO HIM TO
DEFEND THE TOWN FROM APACHE VENGEANCE.

AVAILABLE WHEREVER BOOKS ARE SOLD OR
TO ORDER CALL 1-800-788-6262